DATE D

The Year of the Bloody Sevens

The Year
of the
Bloody Sevens

William O. Steele
Illustrated by Charles Beck

Harcourt, Brace & World, Inc., New York

Library of Congress Catalog Card Number: 63-16036
Printed in the United States of America
First edition

The beginning of another decade of
writing and another round of
dedications—again to:
Mary Q.,
Quintard,
Jenifer,
Allerton,
and to that new family member,
Wilson Gage

The Year of the Bloody Sevens

1

"I'm a-looking," said the man on horseback, "for a feller name of Kelsey Bond."

Kel was startled. Here he was, a-stumbling through the dusk of a March day after the cows, way out here back of beyond nowhere, with not even a path to follow, and up pops a stranger on horseback. And the stranger asks for him by name. It gave him a jolt, for a fact.

"That's me," he squeaked out. His surprise sort of stuck in his throat. "I'm him. I mean I'm Kelsey Bond."

The stranger didn't seem to doubt it. He rummaged inside his shirt a moment. "Can you read?"

he asked at last. "Can you read what's writ by hand?"

"Some," answered Kel. "Pretty good, I reckon," he added, for it was true. His ma and his pa had made all their children learn reading and writing and ciphering to boot. "You just never know," Kel's pa used to say, "when reading is going to come in handy."

And right this minute it looked as though it was going to, for the man pulled a square of folded paper out of his shirt. Kel reached up. The stranger held it at arm's length away from the boy, glancing curiously at first one side, then the other.

"Well, here," he said finally, "this here's a letter for you. Feller up the road asked me to give it to you. I said I didn't mind. Hope you can make it out. Me, I can't read a lick." He spat a long spit into the bushes.

Kel took the letter with an eager hand. He knew what it was. He was pretty sure it was from his pa. He was pretty sure this was the message he'd been waiting for.

"Thank ye," he muttered. "I'm mighty much obliged."

He wished he had something to give the man for

his pains, a noggin of warm milk or a handful of beechnuts. But he didn't have a thing. "I thank you kindly," he said again.

"No trouble." The stranger grinned and clucked

to his horse. He was almost lost among the trees when Tom Every called to Kel.

Quickly Kel stuffed the letter inside his own shirt. He didn't know why. Somehow he just didn't want the Everys to know about the letter till he'd had plenty of time to spell it out and think about it himself.

Tom had the two cows. "Where you been?" he asked crossly. "I figured we was *both* a-looking for the cows. I never had it in mind for me to wade through all them blackberry bushes to get the fool critters whilst you stood here like a calf with the colic."

"I been looking too." Kel defended himself. "A feller riding by stopped me to ask some questions. I'd a-been along in a spell. You ought to of waited."

"Who was it?" Tom wanted to know. "I heared him ride off. What was he after? Did he tell any news?"

"Just some traveler," Kel interrupted quickly. "Didn't know his way around too good. Looking for the trail south, I reckon."

"Don't seem like he'd hardly ride way over here," observed Tom. "How come he couldn't find the trail, plain as it is?"

"He was blindfolded," Kel answered.

For a moment Tom blinked, thinking. "Whatever for?" he asked finally. "How come a man would ride around . . ."

"Listen, Tom," went on Kel, talking fast. "You get on home with the critters. I got a thing to do."

Tom glared a minute with his mouth open, and then he shrugged and turned away. He was younger than Kel and smaller, and Kel had let him know straight off when he'd come to live with the Everys that he didn't want Tom tagging along at his heels everywhere he took a notion to go. Particularly not out here where the Bonds used to live and where Kel liked to come sometimes on his own.

Kel watched Tom following after the cows who were headed home by themselves. Then he looked around. He didn't have too much daylight left. He'd have to hurry, for the place he aimed to go was a right smart piece from here. But it was where he wanted to be when he read the letter.

He set off at a jog in the opposite direction from Tom and the cows. By the time he reached the cabin, he was out of breath. He didn't go too close as he threaded his way through the trees. There were folks living in the cabin, and this time of day they'd be fetching home their own cows and maybe out trying to shoo the hens up closer to the house.

. Still he couldn't pass by without first stooping to peer through the bushes at his old home. Every time he saw it, he felt mighty proud of his father.

15

His pa always did a fine job on everything. When they had come here, his mother had said straight out she didn't want a cabin of round logs that had to be chinked in between with mud. It would be forever hardening and falling out, she said, and that made the cabin drafty. What she wanted was a place that would stand for a long time, all snug and tight against the weather.

"And she got it," Kel said to himself.

The shingles were seasoned oak, thick and well-lapped over each other and pegged down tight. The walls were of logs that had been hewn on the top and the bottom so that they fitted against one another, flat with no space in between. There wasn't a crack a snake could run his tongue in.

Kel shifted to get a better look at the stone chimney. A little light leaked out in spots along the chimney's edge, where Pa hadn't been able to fit the rough stones smack up against the logs. But it was tarnal little light, Kel noticed.

Folks for miles around declared it was the best cabin in the whole settlement of Wolf Hills. A fine cabin and pretty good land—you might have figured the Bonds were settled for life, right there. But it hadn't turned out so, Kel thought sadly.

16

Now Ma was dead, and Pa was gone; he was alone, and other folks were living in that stout cabin.

A man crossed the cabin clearing, rubbing a whetstone down the edge of his ax blade with a long stroking motion. The door suddenly opened and a woman's voice called, "Make haste with that water!" And here came a tad running from the spring with a piggin sloshing water at every step.

It might have been himself Kel was seeing, back in the days when he and his ma and pa lived in the cabin. Three years they had stayed here, and he had helped to clear the big fields beyond the house and to plow and plant the corn. Then an old friend of Pa's from these parts, Benjamin Logan, had begun a station across the mountains to the west and had sent back a call for help.

Pa said he was honor bound to go help Logan. Anyway, the land in Kentuck was by far richer and better than that on their farm. He promised to build a bigger and finer house at Logan's Station and to send for them when it was ready. And after last spring's planting he had gone.

Kel sighed, turning away. They had had a good life here, the three of them, and now it was every bit over. Every bit.

He circled off toward the spring. It was plumb dark down there in the hollow under the trees. He could hear the water's soft murmuring voice, and he knelt and scooped up a handful of the icy stuff and drank it. Then he hurried down the hollow alongside the stream, remembering to walk carefully around the hole where he had dug out the groundhog about this time a year ago.

And, too, he remembered the low place ahead even before he heard the shrill little voices of the frogs. Cold as it was, they were hollering their fool heads off. When he was close to the mire, the frogs were suddenly silent. Only after he had passed and they knew he was going away did they start again, first one and then another, until once more the whole caboodle of them was yelling.

He was running now, across an old cornfield to the hill. The sun had set, and only the fat buds high on the poplars were still touched by its red light. He began to climb. When he at last reached the edge of the crab-apple thicket, though it was dim, he could make out the cedar slab there. He had carved it himself two months ago, not sure of the way to spell things and making half the letters crooked and tumble-down looking:

Sary
wife of J. Bond
dyed 1777

Kneeling, he ran his fingers lightly over the letters. It had been easy to carve in the soft cedar wood. It was just that the whole thing had turned out to be harder than he'd counted on.

Mrs. Every hadn't wanted them to bury his ma way up here. "Hit's such a far lonely place," she said. "There ain't a field or a farm cabin in sight from that side of the hill."

But Kel had wanted it. His mother loved the crab-apple thicket, the mass of pink blooms in the spring and the air so thick with the sweet smell of them that it was hard to get your breath. And then in the summer the little low trees heavy with tiny apples that reddened slowly and clung to the trees long after the leaves were gone. They were there till the juice-drunk wasps died of cold, clean up till Old Christmas, when the squirrels finished up the last of them.

Now, seeing the sprangle of bare black branches against the darkening sky, Kel thought maybe Mrs. Every was right. It *was* a far lonely place. He jumped to his feet. That was foolish. His ma had said she'd like to be buried here. And cold and bare as the place now was, spring would get here, the way it always did. But when it came Kel would not be here.

He reached inside his shirt and touched the letter. His father had sent for him, he knew. And this was his last visit to his mother's burying place. It was why he had to read the letter here, a sort of fare-thee-well before he went on his way to Kentucky.

Why had the letter been so long coming?

Every day since his ma died he'd expected the message. He didn't know how it would come, but it had to come, he knew. Some days it had seemed as though he couldn't stand the waiting. He'd just have to head out alone and make the journey to Kentuck. But he hadn't. He'd waited. It was what his pa had told him to do before he left. No matter what happened, Kel was to stay till sent for. He'd remembered and obeyed, for his pa had good reasons for everything he did. Still and all, Kel reckoned he should have been told to come long before this.

Perhaps his father never got the message about the burying. Perhaps he still didn't know. Oh, he knew Ma was ailing, she was low and sickly when he left, too sickly to travel the long way to Kentuck, to risk the dangers from Indians and wild beasts and bad weather, or to take on the hard work of helping to begin a new settlement.

That was why she and Kel had stayed behind. Kel had seen something uneasy in his mother's face when Pa left, though she had made no fuss, saying they'd go when she was well and Josephus wanted them. But Kel hadn't thought she'd die, not at first.

His father had been gone six months before Kel had known his ma was dying. She got thinner and thinner, and even quilting and stringing shucky beans got to be too much for her.

"I ain't up to it," she'd say, and let her hands fall idle in her lap.

And by and by she would begin to talk about her other children; about Kel's oldest brother who'd left home eight years past and never been heard of since; about the next brother, killed by Indians when Kel was still in his cradle; about the daughter who'd run off with a red-coated soldier and gone to live in some big city in Virginia; and about the youngest of them all, the baby sister, who'd died of a fever before she could walk.

21

Kel had cared for her as best he could in that stout cabin. Mrs. Every came over and helped once in a while. Each time she'd urge him to send his father a message, tell him to come home and see his wife one last time. And more than anything Kel had wanted to. He longed to see his father, for Pa would surely know how to make Ma get well, the way he knew everything.

He had about made up his mind to do it when folks started dropping by to bring food and herbs. And they said Benjamin Logan was having a powerful bad time of it in Kentucky, what with hunger and Injun fighting and hard work. The fort wouldn't be able to spare a man like Josephus Bond. Kel reckoned it would be worse for his pa if he had to stay on knowing how things were here. Kel never sent the message. He waited—and hoped.

"A body can't help hoping," he thought now, standing there in the last of the light. It seemed like hope swelled up in a person the way the buds swelled on the trees in spring, willy-nilly.

Way back there just before his pa left, Kel had hoped his mother would get well quick so they could all leave together. He had honed mightily to go, for he had heard much about Kentuck and the game there. But she didn't. And then all through the summer months Kel had kept hoping, over and over, his ma would take a turn for the better. But she hadn't. Since her death he'd spent every waking hour hoping his pa would hurry up and send for him.

Once more he touched the paper where it lay warm against his body. The long winter had just about gloomed him away till he reckoned he was no more than finger-bone size. But now that was over with. He was Kelsey Bond, big as a rick of wood and snappish as a rooster. There was no more cause to fret. Pa knew his wife was dead and that there would be no reason for his son to stay in Virginia. Now he wanted Kel with him and had written for him to come on quick.

Or had he?

Suddenly Kel felt a cold greater and more piercing than the chill of the March twilight. Suppose it was a message to say his father was dead or Injun-captured or something terrible? The handwriting on the front hadn't looked like his father's, sure enough, now that he came to think of it. It was somebody else writing him.

With trembling fingers he drew the letter out and fumbled it about from hand to hand. He'd been a fool not to read it right away, even in front of Tom Every. Now it was too dark. He'd have to make a fire.

Quickly he raked together some twigs from under the crab-apple trees. He felt around till he found some dry grass. He took a flint and steel from his shirt and made a fire, sheltering it from the night wind with his body. Carefully he fed the twigs to the burning grass. Then in the tiny flickering light, he ripped through the seal, spread the letter on the ground, and began to study out the words.

2

Kel sat on a log at the edge of the trail. He'd been there a right good spell. It had been pitch dark when he left the Everys' cabin and had come stumbling here to find a place to sit. And now the sun was up and the birds were singing. Birds were as noisy creatures as he could think of. That red bird was the worst of the lot. It sat there hollering loud enough to split his ear pans.

He threw a stick at it, and it flew to the top of a scalybark for one last whoop before disappearing. Now he'd be able to hear the cows and folks when they came down the trail. Twice already he'd jumped up thinking he heard them. After that

25

he'd made up his mind not to move a whit, not even when he saw them come swinging around the bend yonder. He'd just sit here, ramrod straight, and not let on he'd been so anxious to meet up with them. And he'd been more than anxious, for the letter *had* been from his pa, though someone else had written his name on the front. It had told him to come on to Kentuck, that Josephus Bond needed and wanted his son with him.

The thought of that letter warmed Kel to his toes. It wasn't every boy in the world who had such a good man for a father. Nor every boy who knew his pa loved him.

"Come ahead the best way you can," the letter read. "The Everys can fix matters for you."

And so they had. And now he was sitting here on the lookout for those "matters." For a fact, though, he wished he hadn't waited. This path twisting off through the trees led to Kentucky. His pa had traveled it back and forth a heap of times, and Kel had never heard him say it was such all-fired hard going. It surely wouldn't take much for a boy near about twelve to follow it. Not a boy who'd been in the woods all his life. Even before he could shoot a rifle, his pa had taken him hunting. Kel reckoned he knew just about everything his pa did about hunting game.

Howsomever, the Everys wouldn't hear of it. "Traveling alone, a lad your age!" cried Mr. Every. "You must be addled, boy."

"It's a long journey," Mrs. Every had added, "and it ain't nohow easy traveling from what I hear. We promised your folks we'd take good care of you. And that means getting you to Kentuck, safe and sound."

That had been the end of that. Kel sighed. He doubted the Everys were right. They'd never walked this trail. For a fact, they'd been living on their farm for close to ten years. What could they know?

Pa had said for him to come on the best way he could. Well, striking out on his own was the best way, he figured. He stood up and stretched, shivery with excitement. He yearned to be in Kentuck right this very minute. And he could see himself at the fort wall shooting calmly away at redskins. Oh, his pa was going to be mighty proud of him —a boy his age holding his place without a thought of danger and never so much as flinching during the Indian charges.

27

He sank back on the log. His pa meant for him to journey with somebody, he knew that well enough. But if the folks didn't hurry up, he'd never get to Logan's Station and have a chance to show how he could handle a rifle. He didn't much hanker to drive cattle to Kentucky. But one of the men was some sort of kin of Mrs. Every's. They'd be glad of an extra hand, she told Kel. With the cows along they'd have food a-plenty, and his help with the beasts would more than pay for his keep.

"That must be them a-coming," he thought, and his heart bumped in his chest. That must surely be a tinkle of a bell. He leaned backward and twisted to peer through the bushes, all goldy-green with new leaves. There, way back yonder along the trail, that glimpse of black and brown and tan bodies, it was cows all right. He straightened up and made his face still and sober.

It was a good thing he did, too, for who should come switching down the trail, along with the bell cow, but a sassy little gal, no higher than his waist, with a long beech gad in her hand and a red-dyed kerchief around her neck. The cow ambled on toward him, but the girl turned and ran back the way she'd come.

"It's him," she shouted importantly. "It's that boy. He's a-waiting by the trail."

Kel was glad he hadn't let on how anxious and stirred up he was. It would never do to show this flighty girl-child. Now he didn't move, except to turn his head and look along the trail the other way, even though he was burning to know how many cows there were and how many folks and what they looked like.

He could hear the girl running back. She stopped in front of him and stood silently waiting. After a minute he turned his head and looked at her. She was tiny and thin with skinny little arms and legs and bright blue eyes. Her hair was the nearest to white he'd ever laid eyes on. She was like one of those little white candle flies that flutter about in the summer evening.

"Here comes my pa," she announced. "He's the one owns all these cows. He's the one a fixing to take us to Kentucky."

Her father was a tall, dark, quiet, worried-looking man. He stood beside her, pulling at his lower lip. Kel got up from his log and wondered what he'd ought to do next.

"Howdy," he said after a bit. "I'm Kelsey Bond."

The man jerked alert and smiled a little. "My name's Henry Worth," he said. "Proud to have you come along. These here cows"—he waved a hand vaguely back at the straggling herd—"these here cows take a heap of looking after." And then he frowned.

There were thirty cows and some other people —Mrs. Worth, who looked as worried as her husband, a man named Fell, who acted a mite simple-minded to Kel's way of thinking, and a tall sullen-looking boy of about fifteen. He stayed back with the cows and didn't do more than nod when Mr. Worth made Kel acquainted with them.

"That there's my brother Clem," whispered the child, pulling at his sleeve. "He's a-sulking, for he had to leave his jularkey. He's feared she's a-fixing to marry up with some other feller whilst he's gone. A body couldn't blame her, could they? He's powerful short-tempered. He don't hardly ever smile nor nothing."

Mrs. Worth was leading a horse loaded down with pots and bundles and other truck. She stopped and almost smiled at Kel. "We're glad to have you go with us," she said.

"Thank ye kindly, ma'am," the boy answered.

Somehow she reminded him of his mother. He reckoned it must be the way she wore her long skirt, all pulled up and belted about her waist. His ma always said she liked her legs free when she walked, not held back by a flapping tangle of skirts.

"We're mighty anxious to get these here critters over the trail and get settled in Kentucky," Mrs. Worth went on. "We got five more young 'uns left back home near Fort Chiswell, and I'm honing to get me a cabin built and get settled afore they come along with the rest of our beasts. I brung this one with me"—she pointed at the girl—"to be a help. And sometimes she is and sometimes she ain't."

The little girl looked up. "I'm a heap more help than Clem," she cried fiercely. "I ain't fell in no creek and got all sopping wet the way he done."

Kel couldn't help grinning.

"No, you ain't," agreed Mrs. Worth. "But I ain't doubting you will afore too long."

She turned to the boy. "You walk on up ahead with her and keep the bell cow going," she said. "I feel better when somebody's tagging along with her." She glanced at Clem, who was having a great deal of trouble with the last of the cows. He laid about him hard with a stick and shouted as if he'd like to kill them all. "But it's them in the back that strays off so," she added with a sigh. And she turned suddenly away and ran after one of the cows, shouting at Clem as she went.

"You want to strap your rifle on the horse?" the little girl asked him. "And not have to tote it?"

Kel shook his head. He'd noticed none of the others bothered with guns, and he figured somebody ought to have one handy just in case. Anyway, he wouldn't feel right without it. He walked through the cattle with the girl, wondering how such a busy little body had ever come to be born into such a sad, weary, glum family.

"My name's Sue," she told him. "Hit's really Susannah, but don't nobody ever call me that. We're named out of the Bible, all seven of us."

"I reckon Sue's a heap easier to say than Susannah," said the boy. "I'm mostly called Kel, myself."

She twisted her head and looked sideways up at him. "Called what?" she asked.

"Kel," he repeated.

She began to laugh. She whooped and giggled,

staggering from one side of the path to the other. Kel caught her by the arm. "Whatever ails you?" he asked angrily. "What you laughing about?"

"I thought you said 'Kettle,'" she gasped. "I thought you said folks called you 'Kettle'!"

He let go her arm. "Well, it ain't that funny," he grunted, but it tickled him to see her take on so.

They walked along in the spring morning. The cowbell sounded sweet and pleasant. The cows' warm breath steamed all around, and every now and then the creatures stopped to crop at the grass clumps or pull a branch from a bush.

"Don't you never hurry 'em along?" asked Kel after a while. "Don't you never go no faster than this?"

Sue stared. "Why, we *be* hurrying," she replied. "You can't make no cow go faster than it wants to. We figure if'n they don't stray too far off the trail, we're going fast. But once they get way out in the brush, it takes a heap of time to get 'em back and headed again. And let 'em get down in a creek! Law me, it can take most of the day to get just one out of a creek, specially where the banks are steep."

Inside himself Kel groaned. He'd be three

years getting to his pa this way. He'd have done better to wait for somebody else to journey west with. He didn't like to fault folks, but the Everys knew he was in a hurry. Whatever for did they push him off on these people?

One of the cows suddenly swerved and trotted into the undergrowth. Its calf bawled and went flopping through the bushes after her.

"Now looky there," yelled Sue. "What's done got into her? Run down yonder a ways and head her back whilst I see if'n I can keep the rest of 'em on the path. Aaiiiya!" She slapped a cow on the flank.

Kel was glad to do it. He needed a chance to stretch his legs. He never had favored walking at a cow's pace. He ran off through the damp woods, and with much arm waving and shouting, he turned the cow and calf back with the others. But no sooner had he shooed her back than another one of the brutes left the trail, and he had to go fetch it.

"Something gets into them makes 'em wander like that," Sue told him cheerfully. "One goes off and the rest just got to follow. It's a pure wonder what they have in their heads."

It sure wasn't sense, Kel thought bitterly. He'd never seen such stubborn, ornery critters in his life. His folks had never had more than two, three cows at one time, and they hadn't acted like these. By afternoon Kel figured he'd already walked to Kentucky three times over, though they hadn't traveled ten miles on the trail. He was tired to the bone and glad enough when they reached a little waterfall with cane all around it, and Mr. Worth said this was a good enough place to stay the night.

Kel leaned his rifle against a tree, waiting there to see if somebody would tell him what to do to help out. He'd like to spread out his quilt and plop down to rest like the cows. Only a couple stood nibbling at the yellow cane leaves. He wondered if he would have to take a turn guarding the beasts tonight. After a day like this 'un, he'd never be able to do it.

He couldn't help feeling sorry for the Worths. It must not be any easy task to travel a long journey with thirty cows, a candle fly of a girl, a sulky boy, and the nitwitted Mr. Fell. It took a heap of worrying and pushing for two people to have the wits of five. He made up his mind to forget how tarnal tired he was and be as much help as he could. He walked toward Mr. Worth, who was driving a stake into the ground.

When he was satisfied it would hold, he turned and nodded wearily at the boy. "Best way I found to keep my cows from wandering," he explained. He rubbed the back of his neck with his hands and frowned. "Stake the bell cow, and the others stay around close. A little salt on that flat rock there and they'll stand here licking it all night. Cows take a heap of fussing and cussing to handle."

"Can I help?" asked Kel.

Mr. Worth shook his head and turned to get the bell cow. Kel reckoned he'd get the wood for the supper fire. But Sue had beat him to it. He went for a piggin to fetch water, but she had done that too. She was scurrying about now, laying out the ashboard for baking bread, scrubbing out the wooden bowls, and somehow stirring stew at the same time. Her skirt-tails swished around so fast and furious they well nigh put out the flames.

Clem fetched up a log that was big enough for a backlog in a good-sized fireplace. Kel was scornful of him for trying to make a campfire out of such a chunk of wood. Clem must have thought so too, for he put the log down and studied it a moment, then sat down on it and glowered into the twilight.

"I reckon Sue's right," thought Kel. "That Clem ain't been much help."

Mrs. Worth was trying to make the cows stand so she could milk them. He grabbed up a cedar piggin and joined her. By the time they'd finished, the stew was ready to eat with hot ashcake and butter. Washed down with a noggin of milk, it made a fine meal. Kel reckoned he might just make it to morning. He chopped some wood, stacked it by the fire, and turned in beside Mr. Fell, who was already snoring away.

Four days later Kel had about given up hope. He'd be an old man with whiskers before he got to Kentuck. He wished mightily that he could see inside a cow's head and figure out what she was going to do before she did it.

"Likely it wouldn't do any good," he thought sadly. "Likely a cow don't even know what she's going to do till she's gone and done it. Even Sue don't know."

If anybody could figure out a cow, Sue could.

She buzzed around them like a spinning top all day long and knew their names and could tell them all apart. Her favorite was a little black spotted beast with a crooked horn and a wicked eye.

"That there's Chrysolite," she explained, "but I call her Chrys, like folks call me Sue. I named her out of the Bible," she went on. "Ma said it wasn't hardly right to name cows out of the Bible, but a schoolmaster, he told me these names out of a little piece of the Bible way at the end that don't nobody hardly ever read. And they ain't names of *folks,* they're names of different kinds of stuff you make walls out of. Some awful pretty names, but Topaz we done ate, and Sapphire fell off a rock, and Chalcedony died of a murrain. That's her calf yonder—watch out, she's a-fixing to run!"

Kel sprinted over and snatched the heifer back onto the path by one horn. He gave her a good prod with his rifle for putting him to the trouble, but she didn't seem to notice.

"And that red one, she's the pick of the herd. She's a Devon Ruby," Sue told him proudly. "Pa sets a heap of store by her. But me, I don't like her. I ain't even give her a real name. I just call her Ruby or Red mostly."

She dashed off as another cow strayed away among the bushes. "Me, I don't like none of 'em," Kel muttered. Why in the nation would anybody want a fool stubborn cow that would just as soon walk one way as another, that couldn't stay on the path and half the time had to be blindfolded and led before she'd cross a creek?

He'd got where he hated the sight of a cow or a piggin of milk, and the sound of that bell nearabout drove him wild. Tinkle, tinkle, tinkle, day and night, slow and steady, and there he was itching to get on to Kentuck, burning up inside to see his pa and help him out every way he could. When he thought Sue wasn't looking, he gave the bell cow a poke with his rifle, and for the next hundred yards she trotted along right brisk.

Well, there was no use sulking. He wouldn't for anything be like that thunder-browed Clem. This fourth afternoon Clem had left to go hunting, claiming he'd heard turkeys gobbling. Kel figured Clem was just tired of stumbling after the cows and wanted to get away. Who could blame him? Hunting was a sight better than this. For a fact, hunting was the finest thing a body could do. In Kentuck he aimed to hunt every single day.

There'd be game there he'd never in his life hunted before and—

There was a shot off to the left. Kel was startled. "That ain't no turkey," he thought. "Turkeys ain't going to come this close to the trail, not with all this hullabaloo going on."

Clem shouted. He was coming closer, and his voice was knife-edged with fear. He crashed through the bushes, and Kel thought, "Something's after him! Injuns!"

The cows milled around Kel, blowing and lowing and tossing their heads wildly.

"Help!" yelled Clem. "Pa, help!"

He came flying out of the bushes, and right behind him came the biggest bear Kel had ever laid eyes on, with blood streaming from one shoulder and froth dripping from its mouth. The great muscles of its forelegs rippled as it loped along. Kel clutched his rifle, half raising it to his shoulder. A wounded bear was the meanest varmint going.

The cows bellowed and ran, here, there, and yon, some toward the bear and some away. Clem fled among them, and the bear never let up but came right on after him. Mrs. Worth screamed, and Mr. Worth fired his musket, trying to get it off the packhorse.

The Ruby cow, which had been running toward the Worths, wheeled and ran the other way. For a minute she and the bear were face to face. She lowered her head and raked it with a horn before she swerved and came galloping on. The bear turned too, quick as lightning. And suddenly there were three cows, with the Ruby in the middle, coming straight at Kel, with the bear close behind them as fast as it could tear.

3

Those big bodies and sharp horns rushing right at him sort of addled Kel's wits. For a minute he just plain forgot he was a boy with a rifle and plenty of sense. He didn't think about anything but what the cows were thinking about, and that was running. He sprinted off through the bushes like a young hurricane.

Somewhere along the way he and his gun parted company, but it was no proper time to stop and hunt for it. He could hear the cows bellowing right behind him, and the cows made sure they could hear the bear. Kel ran harder, but no matter how much he dodged this way and that, he couldn't get rid of them. The beasts favored his company and stuck with him like a tail to a dog.

Somebody fired a shot. It whistled right over his head. He jumped and went faster than ever. It wasn't enough to be chased by wild cattle and wounded bears; somebody was trying to fill him full of lead balls. Oh, if the cows would just choose some other part of the woods to run in, he'd be a sight better off!

Now he was in among some vines that tangled his feet and slowed him to a gallop. He looked wildly around. If he could find a tree branch low enough to leap for, he'd try that. And there up ahead was just what he wanted. He bolted forward and made to spring for the limb, but under his feet there wasn't any ground to jump from, nothing but vines and empty air.

He yelled and clawed out all around him for something to save himself but grabbed only a lot of nothing. He hit bottom with a jolt that sent his heels up into his skull, it felt like. His legs gave way under him, and he rolled over in the mud.

Right away the red cow and the bear joined him in the sink hole, bringing a heaping mess of vines

43

and dead leaves with them. The hole was crowded for three, and Kel made up his mind with no trouble at all that the mannerly thing to do was to get out and let the two of them have it.

The only thing was the Ruby had her foot on his shirttail, and he couldn't get up. He kicked out, and the cow jumped away. Kel scrambled up fast. But he was no more than on his feet before he wished he'd stayed down in the mud. There stood the bear, whopping-big and waiting for him with its arms open and its jaws going.

To his dying day Kel never knew how he got on the other side of the cow, but all of a sudden there he was. The Ruby was bucking and bellowing and tossing her horns about. He had to scurry some to keep her between him and the bear. As the cow swung around, the bear moved out of her way, while Kel circled with them, keeping a sharp eye on both. Around and around they sashayed, like folks at a fiddling.

Then the cow kicked out, and by the yowl of pain Kel knew the bear had been hit. That did it! For a minute the sink hole seemed filled with mad bear. The cow moaned and staggered about. At last the bear fetched her a good clout on the head,

44

and the poor Ruby sank to her knees and toppled over.

Kel was almost pinned under her. He just managed to slide out of the way. He began to pull himself up the wall by the roots and vines. The bear dropped on the cow and bit her in the throat, and she screamed pitifully. The roots Kel was holding snapped. He crashed down on top of the bear. There was a wild thrashing and scrabbling, and he gave himself up for lost. The knife in his belt pressed into his ribs, but he couldn't seem to find it with his hand. Everything he grabbed was thick coarse fur.

The bear looked to have eight feet and three heads. Kel hadn't known there were so many fangs and claws in the whole of the nation. They wrestled around, slipping in the mud and falling over the cow. Finally his fingers found the bone handle of his knife. He jerked it from the sheath and stabbed at the bear, again and again. The varmint didn't even grunt. It just opened its jaws wider than ever, and a whole river of slobber ran out. Now its huge old yellow teeth were right in the boy's face.

Kel screamed then and plunged his knife right

at the bear's head. He saw the blade go through one ear and slice it neatly into two flaps. The bear whooped out a terrible whoop and shook its head. Suddenly it got up and fled. It was out of the sink hole in two bounds and gone.

Kel sat on the ground with his head in his hands. He was terribly winded and shaking all over. Tears of anger and pain and relief streamed down his face. His nose was bleeding, but it hardly mattered with the bear's blood and the cow's blood all over him.

"Boy!" called Mr. Worth sharply. "You hurt?"

Kel lifted his head and looked up. The edge of the sink was fringed with faces, all the Worths and Mr. Fell and even a cow or two were leaning over and staring down at him.

He wiped his sleeve across his face. "Naw, I ain't hurt none," he answered shortly.

But it was a lie. He was scratched and bruised from head to foot. There was a gash on one hand from the cow's horn, and the bear had raked one shoulder with its claws. He could feel the sting of the scratches. They weren't deep, but they'd make his shoulder stiff for a week, he was certain. His

47

shirt was in ribbons across his back, his good deer-skin shirt.

The Worths said nothing more. They just went on staring down. They didn't even offer to haul him out. For a fact, they weren't even looking at him. They were every one looking at the Ruby cow.

Well, she was about as dead as a cow could be. The bear had really laid into her. She looked like she'd already been skinned and quartered, Kel thought.

He stood up unsteadily and raised his head. Not a one of them had moved. Suddenly he was so mad, he near about splintered. "Help me out of here!" he yelled at the faces.

None of this had been his doing. It hadn't been his notion to drive a bunch of fool cows to Kentuck or to shoot a bear just enough to make it fighting crazy or, for that matter, to fall in this sink hole.

Clem reached down a long pole. Kel grabbed it and was hauled up where the wall sloped. Then they all just went on staring.

"She cost me twenty-five deer hides and a keg of

honey and two pounds sterling," Mr. Worth said finally.

"It don't hardly seem much use to go on to Kentucky without a good cow." Mrs. Worth sighed.

"I'm glad it weren't Chrys," muttered Sue.

"I'm glad it weren't me!" cried Kel. "It come mighty close to being me. And it's the Lord's wonder I ain't lying down there dead this minute."

Mrs. Worth drew away from the edge of the sink and inspected Kelsey's back.

"It's forevermore the truth," she said contritely. "I reckon we got a heap to be thankful for. Get that shirt off, Kel, whilst I get some water heated. I got a real good salve that'll doctor you up fine. Won't smart a bit neither. Clem, fetch me some wood."

She bustled about, and her face lost its dazed look. Kel figured she was glad to have something like this to do.

"We'll hunker down here for the night," Mr. Worth told them. "I can butcher the cow, at least get some leather and a meal or two of the meat."

He sent Mr. Fell and Clem and Sue to round up the rest of the cows. It took a lot of doing; they were still skittish and flighty. Kel sat on a log while Mrs. Worth bathed his hurts and spread her remedies over them. The stink was something awful, but he was much too sore and tired to pay heed to a little thing like a bad smell.

Mrs. Worth held up Kel's shirt and shook her head. "It ain't hardly worth mending," she said finally. "Most nigh the whole back ought to come out and a piece of hide put in. Wait till I get my awl and whang-leather unpacked, and I'll patch it for you." She handed it back and asked, "Ain't you got no other shirt?"

"I got a linsey-woolsey," he answered. "But I ain't got no more leather shirt." He unrolled his quilt and put on his other shirt.

Mr. Worth had set some strips of meat to roasting around the fire, and his wife was cutting up other pieces for the stew pot. It began to smell mighty good. Kel wasn't like some folks who claimed tame meat wasn't worth bothering your stomach with. He could eat deer meat or pig meat or turkey or any meat and find it all good. Right now he was glad enough to get his beef collops, and though it might not be as sweet and flavorsome as deer, still it tasted fine enough.

Mrs. Worth wouldn't touch any of it, and her husband said eating it was like eating dust and ashes. Kel felt sorry for them, but he didn't feel sorry for that wobbly-brained Clem, who was eating everything in sight.

"I'm glad it weren't Chrys," whispered Sue on the log beside him. She chewed a minute and then added practically, "Chrys would of been a heap tougher than this."

They'd almost finished eating when they heard other folks coming, the voices first, then the creak of leather and the sound of horses' hoofs. They were camping near the entrance to Moccasin Gap, the only way through the Clinch Mountains. There were no settlements around here, and Kel figured whoever this was on the trail must be coming from Kentucky. Who could it be?

He sat with his mouth open and his piece of ash-cake halfway inside, while a little thrill ran up and down his spine bone. He could sort of halfway make himself believe it was his pa come to meet him.

But it wasn't. It was just folks, travelers like themselves, only headed the wrong way.

"Light and set," called Mr. Worth.

The people halted. They eyed the roasting beef hungrily. "We aimed to go on further tonight," one of the men spoke up. "But we'd be proud to have your company, if'n you'd have us."

"Crowd in," replied Mr. Worth.

Mrs. Worth acted just like a female person who has folks come to stay the night at her house. She settled them all around the fire and served out the stew and got milk for the two young 'uns and made another ashcake.

And it wasn't till they were all through eating that Mr. Worth asked, "Where you all from? And where you headed?"

One of the three men spoke up sourly. "We been to Kentuck, and we're headed for home as hard as we can tear."

A stir went through the Worths. They all looked at the newcomers, as if they couldn't believe what they'd heard. "How come?" Mr. Worth wanted to know.

The man picked up a wood chip and picked at his teeth with a corner of it. Then he tossed it in the fire. "Trouble and more trouble. Mostly with redskins," he answered. "They didn't even wait for winter to get over afore they come around, kill-

ing and burning. We had to stay holed up in Mc-
Clelland's Station for a while. Finally the whole
station give up and them that wanted to stay in
Kentuck went to Harrodsburg. It's a bigger fort.
And we ain't much more than got settled in there
than here come some of the folks from Ruddle's
Fort. They'd give up too."

Another of the men spoke then. "I never even
got to finish my cabin," he said angrily. "I ain't
done no hunting. I ain't even blazed the boundaries
to my land. That ain't no way to live. We headed
out of Harrodsburg the first chance we got."

Mrs. Worth stared at her husband. Her face was
pinched. "Ain't there nobody left?" she asked un-
certainly.

"Oh, there's folks left," replied the first man.
"But a pack of 'em headed home, too."

Kel cleared his throat, and the man looked
around at him. He had to know, but he hated to
ask. Finally he managed, "Logan's Station . . .
it . . ."

The man nodded at him. "It's holding out," he
said. "Boonesborough, too."

Kel sank back with relief. He might have known
Logan's would hold. His pa was there. And he and

Benjamin Logan wouldn't give up, Kel reasoned. They'd stay on no matter how rough it got. Kel could hardly wait to get there and help. They would need him mightily now.

"How about cattle?" Mr. Worth questioned. "Has it been a heap of cattle died?"

The man shrugged. "Them forts ain't big enough for folks and critters both," he answered. "A-plenty cows got left outside, and the Indians killed 'em. Shot 'em full of arrows or clubbed them to death. Indians don't waste no powder and lead on animals."

Nothing more was said. Everybody gazed gloomily into the fire. Kel's heart sank. The Worths had been discouraged enough by the loss of the red cow. Now this news would worry them still further. "They'll turn back in the morning," he told himself. "I just know they will." The thought of going back to the Everys and waiting for some other party of settlers to come by and take him with them made his stomach churn.

But the next morning the Worths set out once again. Kelsey was surprised. "I was sure you folks would turn back," he said to Sue as they started the bell cow off through Moccasin Gap.

Sue skipped off along the trail, poking her gad in and out of the bushes. "My pa said them fellers give up too easy," she told him. "He don't think maybe things is so bad, especially not where we're going. Anyway he 'lows he won't turn back till he knows for sure."

She stopped and shook a shad-blow branch with her stick. As the white blossoms fell, she turned to Kel with a giggle.

"Once my pa knew a feller," she began, "who set out over the trail for a new settlement. Met a feller coming back. Feller says things was bad there, so the man turned toward home. Down the trail a ways he met another man that wanted him to go on to the new settlement, so he turned around and started back toward the new place with the man. When they'd done traveled a day or so, they heard some more bad news, and the feller made up his mind to stop and head for home once again. That feller spent one whole fall sashaying up and down the trail and never did get more than forty miles from home."

She paused, then added, *"My* pa ain't like that. Once he makes up his mind, it takes a heap to change it."

Kelsey nodded. That was a good way to be.

"Oh, ain't it a fair pretty day!" she cried. "Things is so clean and green looking. There's a wild man up in that old sycamore tree. I wisht I had saved some ashcake to eat now."

She walked on, but Kel stopped still to stare up into the branches of the sycamore. His hand tightened on his rifle, for sure enough there was a man sitting in among the patched white limbs. He was wild looking, for certain, a real woodsy with dirty torn clothes and a straggly beard and hair most nigh down to his waist. Only his rifle was polished and fine looking.

"You got good eyes, sister," he called down. "I made sure you couldn't see me up here."

He began to climb down. He was a big man, but he could climb like a coon, and he hit the ground light as a dry leaf. Picking up some gear he had dropped among the bushes, he slung it up on his back.

Sue came back to stand beside Kel. The stranger turned to her. "But you wasn't so sharp-eyed when I passed your camp early this morning. You was sleeping hard, for a fact, you was."

"Where you headed?" asked Kel quickly.

"What was you doing up in a tree?" Sue asked at the same time.

The man laughed. "You two packed full of questions like a chestnut full of meat," he said. "I was up in that tree trying to get me some doves' eggs. A dandy spring tonic, doves' eggs. Clears the blood of winter effluvia. But them eggs"—he jerked a disgusted thumb toward the straggly stick nest in the sycamore tree—"them eggs is done hatched."

He twisted his finger in his beard. "I was a-looking for my partner, too," he added. "Me and him's headed for Kentuck, you can bet. We parted company, and he went off to rustle up some meat. Couldn't see him up there, though. Oh, well, he'll be coming. I'll junket along with you folks for a spell."

"Mighty glad to have you," declared Kel, being polite.

"What's your name?" demanded Sue, not bothering with manners.

"Ben Horne," answered the man.

"Where you from?" she asked next. Kel wanted to tell her to shush; a body shouldn't pester a stranger right off with such questions.

"I ain't from nowhere partic'lar," the woodsy said. "At least most of me ain't. This scar"—and he pointed to his cheek—"it's from down in Chickamauga country. An Injun's knife. This knot, now, on my wrist, why it come from up in Pennsylvania. But since all of me is right here, I got a question for you. Bet you can't answer it."

Bending over Sue, he asked, "What's black as charcoal, sleek as a mole, has a great long tail and a thundering hole?"

When Sue shook her head and said she didn't know, he straightened up, delighted. "Well, there's some more of it. Might help you out," he told her. "Goes this way—long tail, brown feller, pull him back and make him bellow."

Once again Sue shook her head. The woodsy grinned from ear to ear. "Why, hit's a rifle-gun like my Long Jim here," he cried, holding it up. "It . . ."

Somebody on the trail behind them called. He turned and looked back. "That's my partner, old Hoke Carr, a-calling," he told them. "He's fell in with your pap, I'll vow. I'll just go have a word with 'em." He set off back the way they had come through the gap.

Sue watched him down the trail. "Them old riddles," she exclaimed scornfully. "I knowed them both. I knowed the answer was rifle. I just let on like I didn't know so as to be neighborly."

But Kel scarcely heard. He was thinking. If these two woodsies were headed for Kentuck, they wouldn't turn back because of Indians or a dead cow. They would have good reason for going, and they would travel fast, most likely. He just might leave the Worths and travel the rest of the Wilderness Trail with Ben Horne and Hoke Carr. He just might!

But would they take him along? He pondered. Would they be willing to have him? He watched the bell cow picking her slow way through the trees. They had to take him, they just *had* to.

4

"Git up, boy," Ben Horne said harshly. "If'n you aim to journey with us, you best rouse yourself." He shook Kel's shoulder, and Kel cried out.

The man vanished into the shadows, and Kel sat nursing his shoulder where the bear scratches were fiery hot. His whole arm was sore and stiff. He didn't know how he was going to tote his bed pack all day long. But he aimed to, no matter how much he ached.

In a spell he shuffled barefoot over to the fire. There was a little gourd full of salve sitting there hotting for him. Mrs. Worth was kindness itself; she must have got up and put that there for him earlier. He took off his shirt and smoothed the greasy stuff over the hurts and warmed his back by the flames. He moved his arm to loosen it a bit, and then he put his shirt on again.

Kel sat down to slip on his moccasins. They had been by the fire all night and were dry all through, for a wonder. But they were oak-hard. He had to work the leather with his fingers till it softened up a mite. He was wrapping the long laces round his ankles when one of the cows swayed into the circle of light. She stared at him, and Kel grinned at her. She had a crumpled horn. Was it Chrys?

No matter. He was leaving, and he wasn't sorry to say good-by to any of the cows, not even Chrys. It didn't grieve him to say good-by to any of the Worths either, though he figured he might miss Sue. Her busy ways and cheerful talk had helped a heap when he'd been poking along slow with the cattle, but now he was eager to get along the trail.

He glanced over to where she lay sleeping, curled up like a ground squirrel. Last evening he'd sat whittling by the fire and had turned a piece of ashwood into a tiny piggin, handle and all.

Reaching into his quilt, he pulled it out. Then he stepped over and laid it beside the little girl's cheek.

"There," he said softly. "That's for keeping me company these few days."

He heard Hoke Carr and Ben Horne moving around out in the darkness, and he made haste to snatch up his breakfast, cold ashcake and leftover beef stew. He was going to miss that warm milk morning and evening, for a fact.

Kel could hardly believe he was really going. At first he'd been sure the two woodsies wouldn't have him. It had taken all his grit to go up to Mr. Carr and ask if he could tag along with them. The words stumbled out while he tried to tell that he wouldn't be a hindrance to them, he'd keep up good, and he'd hunt his own food. Hoke Carr had interrupted roughly, "Come, if you've a mind to. I seen how good you take care of your rifle. That tells about a body, that does. I don't reckon you'll botherate us none."

It had been as easy as that. But then Kelsey didn't know how to tell the Worths they were going to have to get along without an extra hand. They needed his help; that Clem was no good and Mr. Fell not much better. They might feel Kel was obliged to stay on. He'd have to do some talking to make them see how much more his pa needed him.

But when he had finally stammered out his news, Mr. Worth hadn't so much as batted an eye.

"We'll manage," he had said. "We got along before you joined us, and I reckon we can get along now. Seems to me you're right to go with them. They'll go a heap faster than we can, and I figure your pa's right anxious to see you. It may just be I'll find some other body willing to travel with us."

"I'll stay with you if'n you want me to," Kel offered. He sounded weak and halfhearted, he knew, but it was the best he could do.

Mr. Worth shook his head. "You'd best go 'long," he told him. "If we meet many more folks with bad news about the Indians, I aim to head back home. I ain't letting my cows get stuck full of arrows. If'n you're set in your mind to go on, you'd best go with them."

So now he was going. He tied his quilt into a bundle for carrying. Inside was his torn leather

63

shirt and a pair of wool stockings his ma had knitted. They were big and loose, and he only wore them in bad, cold weather.

"Boy, you ready?" called Ben Horne softly. "We're fixing to skeedaddle. Don't lag, for we can't wait for nobody. It ain't our nature."

Kel gathered up his belongings. As he stepped out of the firelight, a cow brushed against him and blew out her breath in a snort of surprise. He swung his bundle at her.

"Fare-ye-well, bossy," he murmured. "You'll eat my dust this day."

He had a piece of roasted meat he had counted on saving till later, but he was so hungry, he bit off a piece now. He reached the trail and found the two men waiting.

"Here I be," he said, his mouth full.

"Boy, you eating?" asked Ben Horne. "Don't you know it'll give you the colrabbles to eat whilst you're walking? Swallow it on down, quick."

Kelsey choked down the meat as best he could. Mr. Horne had a heap of other notions about food, and he shared them right then and there with the boy. How you must never cut ashcake but break it, else it's bad luck. How if you drop a piece of meat you're eating on the ground, your next rifle shot will misfire.

"And a body ought never to eat anything green before the sun goes down the sky," Mr. Horne went on. "In the early morning, green things don't set well."

Mr. Carr was quite a spell ahead of them when Mr. Horne seemed to run out of things to say. He sprinted off to catch up with Mr. Carr, and Kel hurried along too. But he didn't walk with them, he stayed a few paces in the rear.

Once he looked back, but he couldn't see the Worths' fire. He was really on his way.

At the first creek they crossed Mr. Horne had a drink. At the second and third streams he stopped for water too. Each time he stopped, Kel stopped with him. He didn't know why. "You got a powerful thirst," he observed finally.

Mr. Horne wiped the drops from his beard and shook his head. "It ain't thirst exactly," he explained. "It's just that a body ought to drink every chance he gets. It keeps the joints oiled."

Kel nodded, and for a moment it sounded reasonable. But the more he thought about it, the less sense it made. Finally he gave up trying to puzzle it out.

It was much lighter now, and he could see they were traveling down a narrow gorge between

two ridges. Poplars in pale new green marched up the hills. A little creek ran through the gorge. Sometimes the travelers splashed down the creek bed, and sometimes they moved beside it.

The woodsies walked fast. They were the best

walkers Kel had ever seen nearabout. Still and all, they didn't make too good time, what with Ben Horne stopping so often and Mr. Carr's fits of temper. The least little thing set him off. Let a branch slap across his cheek and Mr. Carr went

into a terrible rage. He would slash at the branch with his hatchet till there wasn't a splinter left.

Maybe it came of having to listen to Mr. Horne's foolishness all the time. Kel reckoned he'd have to take mighty good care to see he didn't cause the man to fly off the handle that way. He'd a heap rather put up with Mr. Horne's silly whims any day than Hoke Carr's cross-grained ways. But it was no wonder these two traveled by themselves. Likely decent folk couldn't stand having them around.

He shrugged. It wasn't any of his business. What he wanted was to get to Kentuck. All he had to do was keep going and try not to step on anybody's toes. He walked on, keeping the men in sight, but not staying too close. Not long after sunup they reached the Clinch River.

Kel stood on the bank staring at the swift current. He waited to see how they would cross. He hoped it wasn't swimming.

"Is it deep?" he asked anxiously at last, for it looked deep to him, deep and roiled and bad-tempered.

Mr. Horne gave him a measuring look. "It's up a mite," he answered. "But there's a rock ledge clean across it. Stay right on that and you won't have nary a bit of trouble."

The woodsies walked into the water like it wasn't there. Kel followed, biting his lip to keep from crying out at the cold. He put his feet down as though he were walking on eggs and stuck to that ledge like a bur to breeches. Sure enough the water never came higher than his shoulders, and that only in a couple of places, but the water tugged at his clothes like a live thing. He was happy to reach the other side.

They didn't stop to dry but sloshed right on and were soon climbing the steepest, rockiest ridge Kel ever saw. He struggled along in his wet clothes. Once Hoke Carr glanced around at him and grinned. Kel pulled his face into a grin, but he didn't feel much like grinning back, for a fact. He was dropping further and further behind in spite of all he could do. Yet he wasn't fixing to ask them to slow down or give him a hand with his bundle. He'd keep up or die trying.

They went over the ridge and down the other side, and there at the foot was a marshy place around a salt spring. The men had stopped, and their gear was spread on the ground. When Kel came up with them, Mr. Carr was gathering wood while Ben Horne checked his rifle.

"Like to come hunting?" Mr. Horne asked. "I

make it a rule to hunt at every salt lick along the trail. I done always had good luck as a hunter and that's how come."

He knocked the powder out of the firing pan. Taking a twig, he poked at the touchhole to clear it of caked powder grains.

"No, thanks," Kel replied. "I reckon not this time. Ain't you got meat?"

Hoke Carr laughed shortly. "*Meat* don't make no difference," he answered. "It ain't *meat* Ben's worried about."

"It ruins a body's luck to pass up a good opportunity like a salt lick," Mr. Horne explained cheerfully. "And once you shot game at a lick, you're honor bound to stop there and try your hand again." With that he turned and trotted off through the buttonbushes.

Mr. Carr gave the boy a sour look. "Ben shot him a big ole bull elk here once," he explained. "Now he's got to hunt here or he'll get fitified." He grunted. "We can dry out whilst we wait for him to get it out of his system."

Sitting down was a thing Kel meant to enjoy. He slumped to the ground and let his bundle slide off his back. He was still panting a little, and he hoped

70

Hoke Carr didn't notice. The climb wouldn't have been so hard, only his wet clothes burdened him, and he had to favor his hurt shoulder and keep the pack off it. Otherwise, he could keep up with anybody; he knew he could. His pa certainly wouldn't like folks having to slow down for him.

A few minutes later there was a shot, and then just a breath after, another shot. Carr cocked his head. "A deer maybe," he said. "Ben's a good shot. He don't hardly never miss."

But when Horne walked up, he was empty-handed.

"Where's our meat?" asked Carr scornfully. "Or be you waiting for me and the boy to go back and fetch it for you, like a couple of Injun women?"

Ben Horne scowled. "My rifle must of got ram-shackled during the night," he answered crossly. He looked it over carefully from end to end. "They was both easy shots, and I missed consider-able on both of 'em."

"Your rifle's been witched," jeered Carr. "Mr. Fell, that simpleton with the Worths, he done put a spell on it so it won't shoot good."

"Shut your jaws," snapped Horne. But he looked

at his gun again and mumbled something to himself. The next time they crossed a stream, he not only drank out of it, but he also plunged his rifle into it and let the water run through the barrel.

Kel had always heard that was a way to take the spell off a rifle. Howsomever, he didn't hold with spells and witches. His pa had told him that was a lot of foolishness. And poor Mr. Fell didn't have sense enough to know a spell from a stack of frog eggs.

For three days they pushed along. They whipped over a couple of mountains, and Kel had to set his teeth and lean hard to keep up. The men could travel up a steep grade as fast as they could go on level ground. It was Mr. Carr, for all his bad temper, who took pity on Kel.

"Don't sprain a leg keeping up with us," he told Kel, dropping back one morning to walk beside him. "The trail's easy marked here to Cumberland Gap. It ain't more'n a year or so since it was fresh-cleared. Widened some too; wagons even been over it. If me and Ben get a mite ahead, you won't have no trouble catching up. We stop every few miles; you seen it."

Kel was kind of taken aback to have Mr. Carr

say this. He'd stayed right with them so far. He hadn't slowed them up none.

"I can keep up," he said fiercely. "It ain't that hard."

Carr shrugged. "Suit yourself," he replied, and loped ahead to join Mr. Horne.

What Hoke Carr had said was true. The two walked fast, as if they were in the dearest hurry to get to Kentuck, but any little notion that took them could mean they'd spend hours away from the Wilderness Trail. They'd journey miles up a hollow to look at some good spot for setting up a mill or a monstrous big tree or a place where they'd heard a man had been snake-bit or wolf-bothered.

Kel was always glad enough to stay on the trail and wait for them. What did he care about a piece of lightning-struck wood that'd keep off rheumatism or an acre of good bottom land?

And right now, Kel thought, from the way Mr. Carr was pointing and waving his arms around, he was going to get another resting spell. Sure enough, they stopped, arguing loudly.

"It was right around that part of Walden's Ridge there." Mr. Horne raised his rifle and pointed. "I remember Manker used that wrinkled knob yonder as a landmark. The silver mine can't be more'n two-three miles from this spot." And he slammed down the butt of his rifle to the ground.

Carr shook his head. "Naw, you're wrong," he said, his voice rising. "That knob is just the first sign. What you got to do is turn off here and head for Powell's River and keep up it to a big grove of sour gums. That's where Manker found the mine."

"I recollect them sour gums," agreed Ben Horne. "But I'd stake my life it was under that high knob yonder."

They didn't say "boo-turkey" to Kel, just set out toward the mountain knob at a trot. Kel squatted in the trail and rubbed his aching calves. Suddenly Mr. Carr stopped and studied the ground. His head darted this way and that. He spoke to Horne and turned back toward the boy.

"You stay right here," he ordered. "We won't be long. But don't you go on ahead. There's Injun signs here. They're old, but it don't pay to take no chances."

He was off before the boy could even nod. Kel didn't mind. He hadn't aimed to do anything but rest here anyway. He stretched out with his quilt under his head. It was a sweet warm April day, and the sun felt good. He lay there like some old snake sunning on a brush pile. He was half asleep when he heard a rattling sound in the bushes.

His eyes popped open. Somebody was coming, somebody who was trying mighty hard to be quiet and surprise him.

"Injuns!" he thought, sitting up suddenly. In spite of the sun, he turned cold all over.

5

Kel reached out and snatched up his rifle. Rolling over, he slid over the rough ground on his belly until he'd managed to put a tree between him and the noise. With his gun across the roots, he stared out at the spot where he had last heard the rustling. He took in every bush and weed patch. Not a thing moved anywhere. He glanced back into the woods, but he couldn't make out anything in that dark, greeny stillness.

He shifted uneasily, wondering if he hadn't imagined the noise. Perhaps it was only some animal, a fox or a 'coon curious about him. Still he waited and watched. There! Over there the bushes swayed ever so little. His hand moved to the trigger. He held his breath, and his eyes bored into the spot.

And right there above some dried seed pods was a patch of skin with one black eye staring out. It was an Indian! His heart thumped around in his chest like a bee in a bottle. He'd never in all his days shot a redskin. Last year's raid at Wolf Hills was the onliest chance ever he'd come close to having, yet the Cherokee warriors had passed his cabin by without so much as raising a war whoop. He didn't reckon he needed any practice. Likely it was no harder to shoot an Indian than any other varmint of the woods.

Now he thought he could make out the rest of the head among the leaves. His fingers trembled. Carefully he eased the front bead sight up till he had it and that black eye in the curved notch of the rear sight. He would get in one good shot anyway.

Then the rest of the man's face came into view, sticking out of the bushes. It took him a minute and a couple of good hard squints to recognize Ben Horne. Kel was so surprised to see the woodsy, he well nigh went on and pulled the trigger anyhow.

Mr. Horne stared across at him with a face like stone. His eyes were as dark and unwinking as

77

any Indian's. Kel stared back, too startled still to do anything else. The man shook his head, a tiny shake the boy could hardly see, and laid his finger on his lips. Then he beckoned him to follow.

Kel gathered up his gear in a hurry and went after Horne. They circled wide, and when they finally came out on the trail, Hoke Carr was there waiting for them. Neither of the men said a word. They just set off down the path at the fastest pace they'd gone yet.

Kel didn't waste his breath asking questions. He knew he could ask till his toes sprouted feathers and they'd never answer him if they had a mind not to. He'd never know whether they'd found the silver mine or not or what had made Mr. Horne sneak up so quiet like to get him. He hurried along with them, but every now and then he couldn't help glancing back over his shoulder. The trail meandered off behind them, empty of any living thing except little yellow butterflies.

Only once, looking back from the top of the ridge, Kel saw three buzzards tipping and rocking in the clear air. Their bare red heads gleamed in the sun. What were they after? An Injun? A bear carcass? Or something else that sent the three of them hurrying along the trail?

He shrugged. There were a heap of things he'd never find out about in this world, and this was one of them, for sure.

The rest of the day they fairly flew along. Kel was glad to be making good time, but he was afraid he was going to die of weariness before they stopped. He hasseled and panted up every hill, his legs cramped, and he seemed never able to get rid of the stitch in his side.

Before the end of the day the Cumberland Mountains loomed ahead of them. In the folds of the hills the deep blue shadows lay like water, and all around the country rolled in easy slopes and shallow valleys. Good farming country, Kel knew, by the beech trees and the thick brakes of cane.

They camped off the trail, and the two woodsies were as silent and stand-offish as they had been all day. But they didn't seem jumpy or worried. They built up a big fire and set no watch. Kel rolled into his quilt. If they weren't fretting over danger, neither was he. He slept soundly.

The men behaved the next morning as if the day before had never been. They jollied Kel about all kinds of things—how long it took him to get his moccasins softened up, how the smoke from the fire seemed to follow him around like it was tied to him with a string, how he dropped his collop of meat in the leaves and ate it with a Betsy bug stuck to it.

And Ben Horne went back to drinking out of every run and branch they crossed till Kel thought it was a wonder he didn't drown. One thing though, they kept to the trail and didn't wander off to look at some googaw.

They passed within hailing distance of Martin's Station. The gate to the stockade was open, and smoke streamed from one of the cabin chimneys, but there wasn't a sight of anybody. A hen clucked somewhere inside, and Kel thought he heard a door slam.

The woodsies tore on past without even glancing at the fort. Kel was glad. He hoped to keep this swift pace.

"I don't take to Joseph Martin," grumbled Ben Horne. "Me and him had a bad falling out once about a cow. Don't rightly reckamember what for now."

He scratched his head. "It couldn't of been about *buying* a cow. I ain't got no use for a cow hardly. Though once I heared tell of one that was trained to hunt."

Kel grinned. "It don't seem likely," he said. Not knowing cows the way he did.

Horne looked solemn. "Yep, this here feller trained this cow to walk in amongst a bunch of geese or ducks, even turkeys, whilst he hid along side of her. The birds wouldn't pay her no mind, seeing she was just a cow. And when he was right in the midst of 'em, the feller would let loose with his old blunderbuss and kill half a dozen of 'em."

Hoke Carr nodded. "I knew that man," he declared. "Knew the cow too. She got to thinking too much of herself. One day she was creeping up on some geese, and she turned her head to tell the feller now was the time to shoot, and just about that time he let loose and blowed the cow's head clean off."

Kel grinned again. He liked to hear the men when they got talking like this. It made walking a heap less tiresome.

"Now if'n that cow had had two heads like one I seen in Virginny one time, getting one head blown off wouldn't of made no difference to her," Mr. Horne pointed out.

"Three, four years ago I seen a little new-born colt, only had one head, but it had four eyes, four nostrils, two tongues, and eight rows of teeth. It couldn't nurse, and it died in just a spell," Carr put in.

"I knowed a man once had six fingers on each hand," added Mr. Horne. "He was mighty proud of it, but I couldn't see it did him a mite of good. He couldn't do anything the better for it."

"Maybe he could scratch his head better." Mr. Carr grunted.

"He had the worst kind of bald head," Horne countered. "I never seen him use an ax, and I know for a fact them fingers never helped him shoot better."

He clapped his hand suddenly to his shot bag. "Thar now! I'm most nigh out of lead balls. I had it in mind to mold some this morning. And I plumb forgot!"

Kel dug in his own pouch and brought out a

handful of round lead balls. "Here," he offered. "Have some of mine."

"The boy ain't fixing to wait whilst you melt lead and mold some, Ben," pointed out Carr slyly. "Not this close to Kentuck, he ain't. He figures to hurry you along."

Ben Horne looked down at the shot in Kel's hand. "Well, I wouldn't mind taking 'em, but I'd have to swap you something for 'em," he said finally. "It's bad luck to take lead as a gift. If'n you don't pay for it, you won't hit a tarnal thing."

"It ain't a gift," Kel insisted. "It's pay. I been eating your meat the whole way. And —and you two been good to me. I'm mighty much obliged."

Mr. Horne rubbed his chin. "That's right," he said. "I reckon it's proper pay." And he took the balls and slid them into his pouch. Later in the day he shot a turkey. "That was one of your balls," he told Kel. "So you was right to give 'em to me, and I was right to take 'em."

Kel was glad that was settled.

They hurried along the trail, walking long after the time they usually camped, so it was early candlelight when they finally stopped. Kel was eager to get to Kentucky, but he had to admit his legs were shaking and he was well nigh dropping in his tracks. He could hardly stay awake till the turkey was cooked.

Mr. Carr had to shake Kel the following morning to wake him.

"Come on, boy, stir lively," he said. "Today we got the last of our hard traveling, and we'd best lean into it."

Kel leaped up. How could he have been such a sleep-eye? But moving around the fire, dressing and gnawing cold turkey, he knew why. His muscles were stiff from yesterday's hard walking.

Mr. Carr went on. "We got the Gap to get through and Cumberland River to cross, and from then on to Logan's Station it's easy footing."

Then they were off, and before Kel could get good and awake, they were climbing the steep side of the mountain to Cumberland Gap. All his life, nearabout, Kel had heard tell of this pass. Folks had talked about it like it was something wonderful, some bright shiny marvel a body could see from miles away. If there was something great here, he didn't see it, going through. Oh, there were tall walls overhead, split and cracked, with dark freckled places where springs seeped through. But a rocky mountain face was the same most everywhere, Kel figured, especially staring at it from below.

They passed down the west side of the Cumberland Mountains and by afternoon had reached the Cumberland River. It was wide, but it wasn't up. It had been, though, and not too long ago, for the high water marks on the trees were still fresh. They followed a gravel bar all the way over. Underfoot it was crumbly and uncertain. Kel remembered the rock ledge across the Clinch and wished he was back wading that. At last they were out of the water and scrambling up the bank. They stopped at the first good spring for the night.

Mr. Horne threw down his dirty blanket. "I shot me an elk here once," he said softly, staring up at the sky, "and that elk was so big that when my bullet went in one side, it took it a whole day to travel through and out the other side."

And the next thing Kel knew, Carr and Horne were both gone, vanished into the bushes.

"Well, I reckon that makes me the fire maker again," Kel muttered. He didn't mind. He was tired enough without tramping around in the brush after game. And he reckoned he was too excited to hold a gun steady anyway. A few more days and he'd be with his pa. Oh, wouldn't he have a heap to tell him. Just three, maybe four days if the two woodsies kept to the trail.

But in the morning things were in a bad way, Kel saw, the minute he was awake. The men were mean-tempered and sullen. Ben Horne poked about the camp as silent and gloomy as a dug grave, and Carr was in the blackest mood yet. He broke the whang on his moccasin, he pulled so sharp on it. He swore and pulled his footgear off and flung it viciously into the bushes. And the other two had to wait most nigh an hour while he thrashed around looking for it.

At last Ben Horne got up and started off down the trail. Carr came up out of the bushes as red-eyed and swollen-faced as a peeved bull. "Where you think you're headed?" he bawled. "Ain't that just like you? Always holding up things yourself and can't wait two seconds on a body in trouble! Well, lemme tell you, you go two more steps down that path and there won't be enough left of you for the crawdads to find."

Kel believed him. He looked mad enough to

split wide open. Kel and Ben Horne stood silently shifting from foot to foot till Carr found his moccasin and knotted the whang, picked up his truck, and set out down the path ahead of them. They hadn't gone a mile when Ben Horne stopped dead still.

"I done left my lead bar lying on that log," he announced finally. "Reckon we'll have to go back after it."

Carr laughed harshly. *"We! You* can go fetch it. I ain't turning back for you. We done wasted enough time already."

Horne took a threatening step forward. "And who's to fault for that?" he bellowed. "Who done a fool thing like throw his own shoe in the bushes? If'n I hadn't got so discombobulated a-waiting for you, I wouldn't never of forgot the lead in the first place."

The men glared at each other. Carr's face was as red as a turkey cock's, and the veins stood out on his forehead. But Horne had gone as white as the underside of a toadstool. His mouth made a little round black O.

"They're a-fixing to kill each other," thought Kel despairingly. He would have been frightened,

*8*7

except he was too put out. What kind of addlehead-edness would make two grown men stand in the trail behaving in such fashion? His pa would have been scornful indeed of such flighty men.

"I'll go," he spoke up suddenly. "I'll go fetch the lead. You two walk on. I can catch up."

The men stared at him. "That's right," Carr said slowly. "The young 'un can fetch it. We'll stay and wait. I can fix me a new whang whilst we wait."

Kel drew a breath of relief. It was going to be all right. He didn't mind the extra walking. He just didn't want them cutting each other up or even shooting each other.

He turned to go, but Ben Horne stopped him. "I'll take your pack," he said. "Maybe it don't weigh much, but there ain't no use you toting it."

Kel was glad to be rid of it. His shoulder was still a mite sore, and the strap rubbed it. Besides, swinging along the path with just his rifle in his hand, his pouch and horn slapping against his side, he could feel like he was already at Logan's with his pa. It seemed as though he was out hunting in that fair country for supper meat for the two of them.

This was mighty pretty country too, almost flat with great old smooth-barked beech trees all around. Their little new leaves still had a touch of gold in them, and the spring sunlight coming through them made the whole woods glow. There was a patch of bush honeysuckle close to the path, and the smell of it was a double wonder. If he opened his jaws and took a big bite of the air, it would be bound to taste sweet, just from that fragrance.

He found the camp without any trouble. There was the lead bar, on a log, just as Mr. Horne had said it would be. Kel snatched it up and started back. His heels were as light as his heart, and he made good time.

He'd just reached the honeysuckle bushes when he heard a shot. Maybe one of the woodsies had spied a deer. But no, there were two more shots and then a heap of them. He paused, listening. Were they fighting each other?

And then he heard another sound, one that made the flesh on his arms burst out with a million little prickles and the hair on his scalp creep and crawl. A war whoop! The terrible wild cold scream of an Indian brave!

Injuns were after the woodsies. He had to go help!

6

Kel's heart was pounding, and his fingers strangled his rifle. He *had* to go help. He knew it. He was needed. Two men couldn't hope to hold out against a war party. But three guns might.

He could hear the fight plain. The rifle shots were faster. He could tell when the woodsies were firing; they used a heavier charge of powder than the Indians, likely a better grade too. Oh, those two could load and fire fast. Their shots sounded through the forest like peckerwoods rattling on a dead pine. They were going to hold the redskins off till he got there. His rifle would make the difference. With his shooting to help, the three of them could kill every single solitary naked savage.

Only he couldn't get started. He didn't know why. He wanted to go. His legs trembled and ached, and that was all they did. They wouldn't bend. They wouldn't carry him toward the fight, in and out of the bushes so he could come up unbeknownst on the Indians and shoot them down.

Just then he heard the scream, a long, low, gargling sound of terror and agony and despair. The Indians had got one of the woodsies. Sweat sheeted down his ribs and back. The day seemed to darken as though a cloud had passed over the sun and made it hard for him to see.

But one of the woodsies must be left. Kel could still help. There was still time. He could still shoot and kill a heap of Injuns. He might save the one whose rifle he could hear firing now.

He could do it; he *knew* he could. He would make himself run forward, firing as he ran, and scattering the few braves who hadn't been already killed or wounded. He and whichever of the white men was alive could hold out and finally win the battle. He could make his feet move and his trigger finger pull.

Only he couldn't. He was scared. He was too

scared to move. But he wasn't a coward, couldn't be, never had been. Oh, maybe he wasn't as brave as his pa or Sed Cosby back in Wolf Hills, who could pick up a rattlesnake in his bare hands. But he wasn't a coward. If he could only get his feet going, he'd prove he wasn't.

The shooting had stopped. It was too late. Only the howling voices of the red men rang and echoed in the woods. The white men were dead, he knew, or they would still be fighting. *They* weren't ones to give up. Not like Kelsey Bond.

He shook his head. He hadn't known he was a coward. He hadn't ever thought about it. It was a thing a body didn't much figure on. He'd always done what had to be done, and he had had it in mind that he always would, no matter what.

Yet he hadn't been able to. He hadn't been able to make himself help out two friends, two men who'd been kind enough to him in their way. Suddenly he groaned and put his hands to his face and reeled over into the bushes. He lay that way for a spell, not caring that he'd dropped his rifle in the trail or that Ben Horne's bar of lead was sticking into his side. The woods grew still once more. The

Indians were quiet. A bird sang close at hand, a round soft whistle, "Ee-o-lay," and fluttered off when Kel moved.

He ought to get up, he knew. Any moment the Indians might be coming this way. He was a fool to lie here with his feet sticking out in the trail, like a turkey dead for two days. They'd kill him without batting an eye if they came up on him right now. Not that he didn't deserve killing. By rights he should be dead like Horne and Carr. He reckoned he deserved it more than they did. They hadn't run off and left their friends to die at the hands of the savages.

"Oh, oh, oh," he moaned softly. How could he have done such a thing? He pounded the soft earth with his fist and kicked out at the bushes. Then he lay still.

At last he got to his feet and looked grimly around. He wiped his face with his sleeve. The Indians must be gone, trotting on westward to raid and kill around the Kentucky forts. It would be safe to go find the two men and bury them. He owed them that much at least, not to let them be gnawed by varmints. He only had his knife to dig with, but he could dig a shallow grave and pile rocks on it. Or he could find an overhanging bank and cave it in on the bodies, the way he'd heard tell of a man doing once.

With his rifle in both hands he made his way through the undergrowth. He was shaking from head to foot, like that time he had the bad ague chills, but he kept going. Reaching the spot where he'd left the woodsies waiting for him, there was not a sign of them or the Indians. He had to scout around a heap before he found where the white men had made their stand.

He saw Mr. Horne first, leaning slaunchways against a tree. Blood made a kind of shawl over his head and shoulders, for he'd been scalped. His face was all ricked up in a horrible kind of grin where a big piece of his face had been cut off.

Kel gasped and looked away. His stomach heaved, and the woods wavered before his eyes. If'n he'd been here . . . if'n they'd counted on his rifle . . .

He slumped to the ground and let his head hang between his knees till the dauncieness passed. The ground under his feet was dark and wet-looking.

It was blood. He moved away quick, scraping his moccasin along the frost-roughened earth to clean off the stain.

Where was Mr. Carr? He'd have to find him and then set to work. He looked around among the trampled grass and broken bushes. He spied his own quilt ripped to bits and Ben Horne's spider skillet he was so fond of broken in three pieces. And beyond that there was something—something that might be what was left of a hand and arm. Kel went slowly forward and forced himself to look.

He remembered how Hoke Carr used to get mad and slash around at the bushes with his ax. Well, it looked as though the Indians had treated the woodsy the way he used to treat the bushes. He was well nigh cut to ribbons.

Kel stared dully. "I'll have to bury him right here," he thought. "If'n I was to try to move him, he'd come all apart." He shuddered.

Then he took out his knife and began to stab aimlessly around in the ground. Yes, the dirt was loose here. He could do it. It wouldn't be too hard. There didn't seem to be any rocks about, however.

Maybe he'd have to get along just using branches.

He hunkered back on his heels and gazed around. And all at once his eyes lit on something that scared him worse than anything yet. There were the Indians' bundles piled there, all their loot and even a couple of rifles. For a minute Kel couldn't do anything but stand dumfounded.

Why hadn't he seen those things before? The Indians had gone off, likely to bury a dead brave or something. They were coming back, though. They were bound to be coming back to pick up this truck. Right this minute they might be heading this way, from any direction. He didn't dare move. Any way he went, anything he did might show the redskins where he was, and they'd be on him like a hawk on a new-hatched biddy.

Nothing could save him. He was going to be killed, sliced up like Mr. Horne and Mr. Carr, or, worse yet, burned to death slowly over a long day or so. Even being a coward hadn't saved him. He'd have done better to die quick, along with the woodsies.

Then he heard them, talking in high harsh voices off among the trees. They were coming! He turned his head and listened. They were coming along the trail, it seemed. And that was all he needed to know.

He sprang up as though he'd been cocked like a rifle and ready to go off. He ran through the trees, blind and heedless, just going, just getting away. He didn't bother even to hold his arms or his rifle out in front of him. Vines thwacked him in the face; briars tore at him. Once he even ran smack into a tree, looking right at it, and still he couldn't miss it. He staggered back, spinning dizzily, panting and gasping, and pitched into a patch of blackberry runners. He pulled himself out and plunged on, running, running, running.

Finally his legs gave out, and he had to stop. He sagged down on the grass, drawing his breath into his burning lungs in big, ragged swoops. He looked up and around. He was out in the open! The trees had fallen away, and he was here in a clearing with nothing to hide behind but weeds and knee-high bushes!

There was a noise behind him, a soft hissing, swishing noise. He turned his head quickly. It was cane. It was cane rustling back and forth in the wind, a whole great stand of it, stretching as far as he could see.

He looked up at the tops of the stalks where the narrow leaves whispered and tossed in the wind. It must be thirty, forty feet tall, he figured. And some of the stems looked as big as his leg. Never in his life had he seen such a brake.

Something moved at the edge of the woods, and he ducked his head down among the weeds. He reckoned he had made too much noise, left too clear a trail when he ran, and the Indians had followed him. It was foolish of him to try to hide, for anybody with half an eye could see him. He couldn't possibly get away. And he was so tired and sore, he couldn't run another lick. They'd find him soon enough, lying here in the grass.

The cane! They couldn't see him in the brake. He could hide in the cane!

He half fell, half crawled through the grass to the canebrake. Without even looking back, he squeezed in between the thick stalks. His rifle hindered him considerably, and the straps of his powder horn and shot bag kept catching on broken pieces. He pulled the straps loose with a jerk and wiggled on, now sidewise, now backwards, as he squirmed and struggled.

By and by he stopped. This was far enough. He couldn't be seen here by any Indian passing along the edge of the brake. He breathed a sigh of relief and sat, facing the way he had entered and holding the rifle in front of him. If a redskin *did* find his trail and was chancy enough to come in here after him, Kel aimed to get in the first shot.

He sat wedged among the smooth columns for a long time. It seemed like hours and hours. He couldn't hear a thing but his own heart dinging away like a dinner bell and, once, a killdeer flying over screaming. His legs began to hurt where the cane pressed against them, and his shoulders were tight and knotted.

Standing, he stretched. Surely it was safe for him to leave now. He didn't want to be here when it got dark. He began to push his way back through the stalks, taking his time because he was tired. On and on he went till at last he realized something was wrong. He hadn't gone this far into the brake, he knew. There was no patch of sky or glimpse of woods ahead. He must have turned him-

101

self around when he got to his feet. Any which way you looked was the same, just cane and more cane.

He swung around and went back. The cane opened before him and closed behind him with a sigh. The ground underfoot was squelchy and wet. He was so weary, he hardly had the strength to push the stiff stalks aside. Finally he had to stop. This wasn't the way either. He glanced around. There was nothing to see in the dim light, no signs to go by, no blaze marks like the ones on the Wilderness Trail, no nothing.

He was lost!

And then he remembered all the stories he'd heard folks tell—how a man might as well cut his throat as get lost in a canebrake, for death was certain sure. How many a man had died of hunger or snakebite or just pure old age trying to find his way out of a big stretch of cane.

He stood there in the green twilight, trying to keep his head. There was a way out; there had to be. But who could find it? Who could get past the tall stalks and out into the open?

Suddenly the stems seemed to move closer, to press in on him from every side. He struck out with his arms and tried to push them back, but he couldn't. The walls of cane crowded nearer and nearer. He covered his eyes with his hands and collapsed, gasping and choking.

7

He was running, running, running. He had never
run so fast in his life before. Bushes, trees, and Indians whirled by him, faster than he could count.
He was running to save Mr. Horne and Mr. Carr.
Nothing stopped him. On he rushed. Suddenly he
was there. Only it wasn't Ben Horne and Hoke
Carr. It was a bunch of cows. Arrows stuck out of
them like pinfeathers on a baby bird, but they
didn't seem to mind. They just kept on grazing
peaceful as you pleased.

No, no, it wasn't cows. That wasn't the way it
was at all. Anybody knew that wasn't the way . . .

Kel was running, running, running. Everything
blurred by him, he went so fast. Indians kept pop-

ping up out of bushes and from behind trees to shoot at him. He was full of bullet holes, and blood squirted out of him in long, curving streams. Mrs. Every tried to sew him up with a needle and thread. But there was no time. He had to get to Mr. Carr and Mr. Horne. He ran and ran, and at last there they were, standing in the forest. He was just about to yell at them and tell them he was coming to save them when the woodsies suddenly turned and began to shoot at him. The bullets came straight at him, big prickly ones the size of chestnut burs, all red and shooting sparks . . .

He screamed and opened his eyes. Where was he? What was he doing wedged down between these stalks? Why was the day such a curious dim green color?

He sat up and stared at the big jointed stems around him. He remembered now. He was lost in the brake. He didn't know how long he'd been lying here. It must have been quite a while, for the light had changed. The sun was going down. He'd have to try to get out before dark. He didn't hanker to spend a night in such a place.

Picking up his gun, he got to his feet. There was nothing to do but strike out, since he didn't know west from Adam's off-ox. Unless he spat in his hand, hit it with his finger, and then followed the way the biggest blob of spit went. That's what Tom Every always did when he went to hunt the strayed cows.

He pushed his shot bag and powder horn behind him, so they wouldn't snag on anything. He'd get out of here. He wouldn't study about anything but getting out. He wouldn't let himself get scared. He'd keep his mind on that first step and then the next one and the one after that . . .

With his teeth set he elbowed his way into the stiff reeds and pushed steadily on and on. Leaves and stems fell from overhead and stuck to his sweaty face and neck. He tried not to notice how hungry he was or that his mouth felt as dry as a puffball. He just forced himself on, staggering, tripping, as he squeezed and shoved through the wall before him.

The ground underfoot grew soggy and slick. The cane was smaller, hardly as big around as his rifle barrel. And then he was sloshing through a little pool of water. He stopped and drank. It was good. He couldn't get enough down his tight, parched throat.

Cane grew out of the water, and some of it was shorter and younger looking than the rest. And over at one side was a whole bunch of shoots. Cane shoots were good to eat, he knew. Even raw, a body could get along on them. He grabbed a handful and stuffed them in his mouth. They were crisp and not very tasty. Since they were all he had, he ate a lot and picked the rest to take with him in his pouch.

Then he floundered on. It felt queer, pushing along and pushing along and never coming to anything any different. Just stalks and more stalks on every side, before and behind him, over and over again . . .

As soon as it began to grow shadowy, he stopped. With his knife he hacked down a few stalks to give him room and then spread their tops on the ground for his bed. He ate the rest of the shoots. He longed for a fire to cheer him up and to keep off any varmints that might come prowling around. But he daren't. These dry stalks would go up like gunpowder, and he'd be burnt to a cinder in no time.

He settled down to sleep. But he couldn't. He had such a funny hurting up under his ribs. It was hunger maybe. Or else those cane shoots had poisoned him. He twisted this way and that trying to make it go away. But it stayed. Likely he was going to have that pain all his life, he thought miserably a bit later. It was the ache of being a coward, of having failed his friends when they needed him. There wasn't any simple to cure it. He put his hands up to his eyelids and pressed hard with his knuckles to keep back the tears.

"Pa," he whispered. "I never meant to. I never meant to a-tall."

Oh, that was the hard part still ahead of him, for he'd have to tell his pa how he had shamed him.

He must have dozed off. When he woke, it was pitch black all around him. He was cold and cramped. Something rattled off to one side. He stiffened. There was a heap of mean varmints in brakes. Bears came in, the worst kind, wounded bears, with a fierce grudge against every living thing. Monstrous snakes, rattlers and cottonmouths big enough to swallow a man alive. Kel listened so hard, his ears well nigh sprang off his head. He sat up with his rifle ready. What was that and that and that? He never got a glimpse of anything.

Cold and hungry and stiff as he was, he managed

to doze off every once in a while. But any little scratching sound or growl or cry startled him awake. A guilty person always slept restless; he'd often heard folks say so. And he had the heaviest kind of guilt to fret him.

The next time he woke, it was morning. He was raving hungry—and so sore-muscled and aching, he could hardly get his legs untangled. His feet were swollen, and he took off his moccasins and rubbed them.

While he retied the whangs, something moving caught his eye. It was a little lizard, bronzy yellow with two dark stripes down its sides. It came forward slowly and cautiously, and Kel could see little bits of its neck going in and out on each side of its head as it breathed.

Then all of a sudden it fled. It went off like lightning, and right behind it came a snake. Though it was going so fast, Kel knew what it was, a red adder and deadly poison. He backed away. He would have liked to save the little lizard but not at the risk of getting bit. He had troubles enough.

That was a mighty lucky snake, he knew that.

Kel'd give most anything for a meal right now. A piece of bread—he'd sure like some of Mrs. Worth's ashcake and warm milk.

But there was no use thinking about it. He'd be a heap older before he tasted bread again. He'd be

lucky to shoot some varmint to eat this day or come on some more cane sprouts.

He picked up his rifle and began to load. His pa had always told him to load fresh every morning, and he tried to do everything his pa told him. Now he brushed the powder from the pan and took a metal prick from his shot pouch to clean any caked powder grains out of the touchhole. He put fresh powder in the pan and was as ready as he'd ever be, he reckoned. There was nothing for him to do but to set out once again.

It didn't take many steps to see how weak he was, well nigh helpless as a new-born baby. There were places where he just plain didn't have the strength to push through. That meant he had to find a spot where the cane grew more sparsely or the stalks were not quite so big and hard to shove aside.

Still, somehow he managed to stay on his feet and moving.

All at once he stumbled through the cane and out into a clearing. There he stood, looking up with blinking eyes at the blue, blue sky and marveling. He shuffled over into the sunlight slanting across the cane tops and flooding one side of the clearing. Oh, it was warm and comforting. He breathed in great lungfuls of air and stretched and kicked out his legs. He felt as if he'd been tied up with ropes for years and now he'd been set free.

Not that he was out of the brake by a long shot. It still ringed him around. He was like a chicken in a pot. But it was mortal fine to be able to hold out his arms without ramming them against those smooth trunks.

The clearing, he figured, must be close to twenty feet across, a tangle of vines and weeds and buttonbushes. The earth was boggy but no worse than lots of places back in the brake where the stalks grew thick. What could have made such a place, he wondered. No mind, here it was, and here he was, and he meant to make the most of it.

A shadow went over, and he raised his rifle quickly, but he was too late. Whatever it was had gone by. In a minute a marsh chicken came slipping out into the clearing, a thin little striped and freckled bird. But before he could bat an eyelash, it vanished, disappearing among the stems as though it had turned into a leaf.

He wasn't honing to go back into the cane. He might as well sit here for a spell, he told himself. He could catch his breath and maybe get another chance to shoot something. This would be a good place to cook it too, provided he did kill something.

He sat down on a tuft of grass and waited. By and by there was a little squawking sound and a parakeet swooped down and clung to one of the cane stems. It hung there, half upside down, turning its head this way and that.

There wasn't much to a parakeet, for a fact. But a body could eat 'em. Slowly, slowly, Kel raised the rifle and took careful aim at the head. A lead ball could just about tear a parakeet to pieces. He squeezed the trigger. There was the roar of the shot, and the gaudy little bird tumbled to the ground. He ran to it and found the head blown clean off. He could still shoot true and steady, he told himself. At a bird, anyway.

He plucked it quickly, and the bright green and

gold feathers made a gay circle all around him. Susannah Worth would have liked those feathers, might have used them to make a wand to shoo away the flies from Chrys or a cloak for her corn-shuck dolly. With flint and steel Kel built a little fire. Spitting the bird on a piece of green cane, he began to roast it. It smelled so good, he couldn't wait for it to cook. He snatched it off and ate it In-jun-fashion, half of it raw and the other half still so hot that it burned his mouth.

He cracked the tiny bones and sucked out what-ever juices they had in them. He ate every lick of flesh, and though it wasn't much, it was a help. Then he sat back, hoping another bird would hap-pen along.

But none came. Now clouds began to drift across the sky, at first as white and fluffy as the down from a goose's breast. After a while they darkened and began to mass together. The sun was sliding fast down the sky. Kel had to leave, he knew. He had to go back into the brake, and he dreaded it. He didn't know whether he could do it or not. Maybe he could just live out the rest of his life here in this little round clearing with the cane standing back from him and the sky overhead.

At last he staggered to his feet and stamped out the fire. He sniffed the air for rain. Those leaden gray clouds meant showers, he knew in reason. Perhaps it would pass him by. He hoped so.

Turning, he went slowly toward the western wall of plants. Now he knew his direction, and he aimed for Kentucky. He pushed himself inside the dim mass of stalks. Once he looked back over his shoulder at the cleared place. He took another step and the clearing was gone, vanished like the marsh chicken, there one minute and wiped away the next. He yearned to turn around and go back, at least get one more look at that open space. He twisted his head to the west instead and forced his way on through the stiff stalks.

Thunder roared off in the distance. The cane beat now this way, now that, in the wind. The sweat on his face cooled, and his shirt stuck clammily to his back. It was getting too dark to go on. Kel stopped and cut some of the stalks and stuck the top half of them into the ground in a kind of tent-like shelter. With a blast of wind the rain came. It was fierce, but he managed to keep fairly dry. It was black night before the drops lessened to a mist and finally stopped.

He hoped he could get some rest, stuck helter-skelter like this among the cane. He was doubtful. Likely it would be a long, wakeful night. He placed his rifle on one side of him where he could reach it easily. He slipped the straps of his horn and pouch over his head and settled them on the other side.

For the longest time, he lay awake staring into the darkness. He tried to think about cheerful, happy times long ago when his mother was alive and his father was home. But it was a queer thing how a body couldn't order his own thoughts about. No matter how much he tried, his brain seemed to take some roundabout way of its own and always to end up there in the canebrake. When he finally slept, he slept soundly, and it was full daylight when he woke.

He couldn't think why he hadn't wakened sooner. He was lying in a stream of water. A creek must have risen in the night and, freshet-like, was running through the brake. He sat up and reached out hurriedly for his rifle. Snatching it up out of the water, he turned for the rest of his gear. There lay his pouch, washed up against some cane a few feet away. But where was his powder horn? He sloshed and splashed about in the water, feeling everywhere around his shelter. It was no use. His powder horn was gone!

8

Kel stood with the water halfway to his knees and bowed his head. He was going to die here in the brake. He might as well get used to the notion. It was fit punishment for a boy who had deserted his friends and let them get killed by Injuns without as much as raising a hand to help them.

In sudden anger he flung his rifle into the water. He had just reached into his shot pouch to send the lead balls after the rifle when a voice said, "Kelsey!"

It was his pa's voice! He whipped his head around, looking every which way, and he almost called out, "Pa!" But the voice was inside his skull, he knew, not out. It was just the way his pa spoke to him when he wanted Kel to know he was acting the fool.

With the lead still in his fingers Kel stopped and took a deep breath. He watched a little string of bubbles float by and swirl off among the stalks. He wasn't dead yet. He was still lively, for a fact.

"I won't do it," he whispered fiercely. "I ain't fixing to just stand here and starve to death. I'll get out of here. It ain't—it ain't right not to try to save yourself, no matter what bad things you done."

If the bubbles rippled off in that direction, it stood to reason there must be a current running that way. Then there must be high ground the other way. Cane never went far from water that he knew of. Travel long enough away from water and he'd be bound to get out of the brake.

He reached down and groped in the muddy stream for his rifle. He was shamed to think how he had despaired and double shamed to think he'd tried to lose his rifle, his own good gun his pa had given him and that he'd been so proud of. It might not serve him right this minute, but some day he'd have powder again. He wouldn't give up. Giving up was as bad as forsaking people in need.

He waded. It was a sight harder to push through

the cane walking in water. He hadn't gone ten feet
before he was panting and sweating. His feet were
sore, and his hands and wrists were sawed and
cut by the stiff leaves and tough stalks. But he
wasn't going to quit. He'd keep going till he got

out, even if he wore himself down till he was no
bigger than a cane stalk, even if he cut his hands
right off his arms. He *had* to get out. His pa was
waiting for him.

After a spell the water grew shallow, and that
helped. By and by he was slopping through mud,

but there was a powerful tangle of catbrier underfoot and some other vines he didn't know. They tore at his legs and held him back till he was half crawling. He was so busy hacking at them and pulling away that when he looked up and saw the sycamore tree, he well nigh didn't take it in.

He was out! He was free of the canebrake. The big stalks thinned out and scattered, and up ahead were trees and open space!

He could have cried. He clawed his way out of the tangle and left the cane behind. It felt wonderful to be out, and yet it felt queer too. The sunlight was enough to blind him, and the clear air around him made him lightheaded. He staggered over to some rocks and lay down, holding his hand over his eyes. He was grinning from ear to ear. He was out! He'd beat the cane. He'd been right not to give up.

After a while he sat up and took off his clothes and spread them out to dry. The spring breeze was chilly on his bare skin, though the sun-warmed stone under him was as good as a fire. He stared up at the sky. How far a body could see! He'd most nigh forgot how to do it.

When his clothes were dry, he put them back on

and squatted in the sun trying to figure what to do next. He had no notion where he was; he couldn't even rightly remember which side of the trail he'd been on when he ran from the Indians.

It didn't matter. He'd had his fill of trail travel. He meant to stay away from paths and their dangers. Now that he was out of the brake and could tell directions, he would travel west and get to his pa without using the trail; he knew he could. The fort was close by. It had to be.

Howsomever, he'd have to rest a day. His feet were in bad shape, swollen and bruised. They wouldn't carry him far.

Kel gathered up his rifle and shot pouch and began to climb the hill behind him. He didn't like being so close to the brake, and anyway he could see better from the hilltop. And he could camp in that grove of pines.

From the crest of the hill he turned and looked back at the cane. His heart shriveled in his chest when he saw how far the green stalks stretched, a wide river of gently waving leaves meandering off into the distance. A body could be lost in there forever, traveling this way and that, never getting to the edge. Kel had got out, however. And somewhere off to the west was home, all the home he knew now, with his pa. He had to get there, and that's all there was to it.

He stripped off the bark of a pine, tore out some of the inner bark, and chewed it. It was juicy and faintly sweet, but it was stringy and hard to swallow. It would fill him up and keep his stomach from forgetting what it was there for, though it wouldn't stay with him long. What he needed was meat, and he hadn't any idea how he was going to get it without powder.

He knew a heap about what to eat in the woods. His ma had showed him and his pa too, and he had learned well. Berries and roots and buds were some different here than at home, but not so much that he couldn't find something to keep him alive. Still he'd have to have meat if he was going to travel.

All the rest of that day he stayed on the warm pine needles on the western slope of the hill. He got up every now and then to pick fern sprouts or some new young leaves and buds to keep something going down his gullet. Mostly he rested, and that night he slept soundly.

In the morning the swelling had gone out of his feet. He could have eaten a whole huckleberry bush if he could have found one. He wished he could have rocked a squirrel, but he had never been much good at flinging rocks. He ate some more of the gray-green fern shoots looking like coiled-up ropes. Then he made up his mind to set out. If he were going to die from lack of food, he might as well die walking.

After a while he figured he *was* going to die. He just went on walking and walking through the spring woods, past great trunks of trees, oaks and walnuts and sycamores. He went over one creek and another, up one slope and the next, and it all looked the same. There wasn't a sign of any living thing, not even squirrels or wood rats. He was all by himself, clean in the middle of nowhere, in a place where no other man, white or red, had ever been.

He got hungrier and hungrier. Once he found ground nuts and roasted them, but it was the wrong time of year. They were tasteless and so tough that he could hardly chew them. And one time he came on a big patch of strawberries glistening among the grass. He fell on his knees and began to stuff them into his mouth. The sweetness made tears come to his eyes. He'd never tasted anything so good. He ate so many that he was sick and spewed them all up in the bushes. He lay on the ground and rolled around with the pain in his belly.

After a while he fell into a kind of sleep. He could hear voices talking and talking. They said his name and Hoke Carr's and Ben Horne's. They said words like "rifle" and "Injun" and "coward." Mostly they just murmured and babbled endlessly on with a soft, slurring sound, till all at once he thought he was in the canebrake again. He jumped up and cried out. Something scurried away among the undergrowth.

It was morning. He sat with his head in his hands and tried to think what to do. He'd been wandering longer than he'd thought. Strawberries didn't get ripe before May. He'd seen poplar trees blooming, those wide orange and yellow blossoms rising up out of the new green leaves. It was May for a fact.

He'd have to walk faster. Yet he knew in reason he couldn't. It was all he could do to stand up and shove one foot in front of the other. He ought to leave his rifle behind, he reckoned. He could travel faster if'n he didn't have to tote it.

He set his jaw firmly. He meant to hang on to his gun, no matter what happened. What good could he be to his pa in Kentucky without a rifle? He emptied his shot pouch of all but two lead balls. He'd keep those two. It'd be a kind of reminder that some day he'd get to use his rifle again.

He drank out of a little stream and spied some fish in it. He wasted half a morning trying to catch one with his hands, but he couldn't, and staring down into the bright moving water made him dizzier and more lightheaded than ever.

He trudged on.

"I'm lost," he told himself once. "There's something in this world means for me to be lost. I got out of the brake just to get lost here in the wilds. I'd ought to of come on some sort of sign of white men long afore now."

Well, he'd found himself once before, and he'd do it again. He'd have to leave his rifle behind, though. He couldn't carry it any longer, weak as he was. He'd hide it in a clear marked place where he could find it later.

He came to an overhang of rock. One of the rocks was crossed with veins of several colors. The bottom streak was a deep yellow, flashing over the dark rock like a little piece of lightning in the sky. He'd never seen anything so pretty. He hid his gun against that rock and covered it with leaves.

"There now," he said softly. He didn't dare speak out loud; the sound of his own voice scared him somehow. "You stay close there till I come for ye."

He set off through the trees. But his feet dragged more and more. He was lonesome without his rifle. Just the feel of it swinging in his hand was a heap of company, the best there was out in the woods.

Lots of hunters gave their guns names. He'd seen grown men patting and stroking their rifles after a good shot, like the whole thing had been done by stock and barrel. He'd never thought to put a name to his own, though he'd grown up with it, most nigh. He'd figured it was plain silly to act so. But now, suddenly, he felt uneasy and ashamed, as though he'd abandoned his rifle the way he had Hoke Carr and Ben Horne.

Kel turned around and went back. He hated to, his legs trembled so. Yet he pushed on and found the striped rock easy enough. He reached under, half expecting his gun to have got up and walked off. And when his fingers touched it, a little tingle ran through him. He dragged it out and headed westward once more.

It was a bad time of year to be without a gun. Sprouts and shoots had grown up now and were bitter or too tough for his weak jaws to mash up. He ate leaves like a browsing cow and bark like a starving deer. He chomped on green berries when he could find them. He had gotten so thin, he had to tie up his breeches with a grape vine to keep them on.

One day he stumbled and fell and couldn't get up. He pushed his rifle away from him, under some bushes. This time he didn't have the strength to pick it up. He wasn't even sure he could fetch himself up to his feet. He got to his hands and knees but lost his balance and lay for a long time beside his rifle, all twisted in among the bushes.

The scratch down one side of the walnut stock shone plain and white. That had happened the first time he'd gone bear hunting with his pa. Sap green and foolish, he had rushed up to the critter before it was dead, and it had whaled out at him. His pa had said leave the mark there to remind him to be cautious after that.

Kel reached out a finger and traced the deep

scratch. That was a new cock holding the flint. Mr. Every had picked it up for him when he'd gone trading across the Blue Ridge Mountains. Wood and metal, it was a good rifle.

He staggered to his feet. His head reeled and ached, and his feet were two lumps weighing a thousand pounds. He bumped into a tree and went skidding to the ground. This time he couldn't get up. He tried, but he just couldn't. In his chest his heart pounded, slow and heavy.

Slumping over on the moss, Kel lay with his eyes closed and the world going round. After a while he felt better. He squinted at the sunlight where it splotched the woods here and there about him. If he could just see some sign of white men, hear some halloo, he could get up and go on. He knew he could.

There wasn't a thing to show that men had ever walked here. The only sound was a woodpecker tapping somewhere. Or was that an ax? He raised his head to listen. It was something striking wood. Somehow it didn't sound like a woodpecker or an ax. He had no notion what it could be.

Then there was another sound, a horrible sound, a curious high-pitched, gurgling, moaning bleat.

He wished he hadn't left his rifle. He wished somebody was around, any kind of a body, so he didn't
have to face this all by himself, whatever it was.
The noise came again, louder, and Kel felt his hair
creep swiftly along his scalp.

9

Kel was glad he still had his knife. With an effort, he loosened it from the sheath. Whatever was making that noise meant him no good, he was sure. Still he aimed to save his skin by hook or crook. He rolled over into some ferns and waited. The tall ripply fronds scratched his face gently.

There was another flurry of tapping sounds and then the gasping moan again. What in the nation could make a sound like that? It couldn't be a man, could it? It didn't sound human. But it didn't sound like any animal he knew either. What fierce strange thing could be here in the Kentucky woods?

He could remember tales of this land where bones as big as trees lay tumbled about the salt licks, where there were black mysterious caves from which the air breathed in or out depending on the season of the year. A boy who'd gone off and left two white men to die—what could he expect but some bad thing to happen to him? And in this place it could be most any kind of thing.

The sharp rat-tat-tat came again. Tired and dizzy as he was, he knew now that the noise wasn't coming any closer. It was just where it was when he'd first heard it.

He could get away. He didn't have to squat here like a sun-dazed hoptoad and wait to die. He got up on his hands and knees and looked around. He could crawl off behind those bushes. He could get down in that little holler and sneak off.

And then he saw it. It gave him the horrors. A shape, a . . . a big brown body standing up tall against a sugarberry tree. Its arms and legs flailed out as he watched. There were sharp hoofs on the ends of the legs and, as far as he could tell, on the arms too. And the creature had no head!

"It's one of them fluff-headed dreams," Kel told himself. "It ain't a real thing a-tall. I'm making it up."

But he got to his feet and, holding from tree to tree, went closer. What he saw made him near-about faint dead away. He blinked a couple of good hard times to make sure. Then, with his knife gripped tightly in both hands, he ran stumbling forward and plunged it into the deer's neck.

The beast kicked out fiercely, screamed once again, and flung itself wildly back and forth. Kel held on for a moment and then fell, bringing the knife with him. A stream of blood gushed into his face and ran down his clothes. The ground was slippery with it, but he managed to get out of the way.

Holding himself up against a tree, Kel waited as the deer's body slowly wilted against the tree and grew still. The flow of blood stopped. He reckoned it was dead surely. He took his knife and cut off a piece of the warm haunch and thrust it into his mouth. It was tender and good and sweet, and he wolfed it down.

At first his stomach didn't know what to do with it. It rumbled and heaved about in a rambunctious way. After a spell, however, it quit churning, and the world quit spinning around him. It

was a bright and summery-feeling day, and he had meat, a buck, a young one with antlers just beginning to sprout up through its head.

Kel grinned. "You done me a favor," he whispered. "I ain't never seen a deer get its head caught in a tree crotch that way. But you couldn't of picked a better time to do it did you try."

He ate another piece of meat, trying to make himself chew and swallow slowly. The deer must have been reaching for those green pods on the vine winding up the trunk. It must have reached too far and wedged its neck and jaws in between those two big limbs, so it was stuck fast.

"And I done you a favor too," Kel went on. "It ain't likely you'd of ever got out of there. It was a heap easier and quicker to die of a knife than of starving. Or worse yet, of having some other varmint come chew off your hind legs."

Oh, it felt mighty good to sit there and eat, and talk too, even to a dead deer. He almost laughed to think how close he'd come to running away from the thing that would save his life. As soon as he felt a little steadier, he'd make a fire with his flint and steel. He'd cook some of this meat and dry the rest to take with him. There'd be enough here to last him half the summer if needs be. He'd find his pa easy now that he had some meat.

He spent he didn't know how many days right there beside the deer carcass. Daytime he smoked the meat over several fires till it was dry and tough, all the meat except what he ate while he rested, and that was plenty. At night he left only a little fire going. It was a risk, but he had to keep varmints away from his food.

He slept close to the deer and hardly ever dreamed. But some nights it was hard to get to sleep. He twisted and squirmed, remembering back to that day when it all began. It would have been so easy, so easy. All he would have had to do was make his legs go, run with his rifle toward the two men. And instead—he buried his face in his hands. It was a soul-wearying thing to be a coward.

At last his task was done. The deer's skeleton lay scattered around the foot of the tree, and the shreds of meat left on the bones had begun to stink a little. Kel's shot pouch bulged with strips of dried meat. He put out his fires and left without looking back.

He hadn't gone far when it came over him

that something was missing. "My rifle!" he cried aloud and turned around right there.

It was queer he hadn't given it a thought those days by the fire. You'd have figured a body would remember a thing that meant as much to him as his rifle.

He found it without any trouble. It was rusty looking. And something had gnawed on the stock in one place, after the salt from his sweaty hands, he reckoned. Still it fitted his grip mighty easy and rested against his shoulder as comfortably as ever. He could barely remember how just a little spell before he'd been so weak and fainty and his gun had been so heavy and cumbersome.

Later, swinging along among the trees, he reached down and helped himself to what his ma called "nibbles." How had he lived on such all those days? It seemed to him a wonder he was still alive at all. Such truck was only a lick and a promise of food.

He was careful with his meat, eating enough to keep up his strength but filling in the cracks with whatever he could lay his hands on. Berries were ripening now, and once, crouching in a cave on a stream bank after a rain, he saw an old snapping turtle come crawling up the bank to lay her eggs in the sandy earth.

He didn't go near her. He knew about snapping turtles. They were mean varmints with jaws that clamped shut like the gates of hell on a sinner. He waited till she'd dug a hole and laid her eggs. With a couple of swipes of her back legs she kicked sand over them and then lurched back to the creek. He ran down then and scraped the sand away.

The shells were round and pale yellow and leathery. He picked up two and carried them back to the cave. One slipped from his hand. It hit the rocky floor and bounced in the air. Kel's mouth dropped open.

"Too bad hens don't lay eggs with shell like that," he thought. "Then a body wouldn't have to worry about dropping them."

He spent some time letting the eggs fall and watching them spring back up. He chuckled. He wished he could show these eggs to Susannah Worth. It was the kind of thing she would admire to see. Bouncing eggs!

After a spell he split them open with his knife and ate them. They were strong and oily, fishy tasting, like a wild duck's eggs. Two was all he could stomach. Let the rest hatch if they were a mind to.

He set out again. There was a heap to see now that he was full and warm and didn't have his mind on his belly so much. Springs with water as blue as indigo, old beaver dams half hidden in cattails where the red-winged blackbirds swayed and called, meadows with sweet-smelling clover, and sometimes, off across an open place, the big, dark, high-shouldered shapes of buffalo. The sight of them made him tingle with excitement and grip his rifle hard.

"A smidgin of powder, just a palmful," he thought with a groan, "and I could kill my very first buffalo-critter."

Sometimes he talked to himself, for it was mortal lonesome. There was this to say for being so hungry that you were flighty-headed; you had a brain pan so full of voices and noises you never noticed how still and solitary it was.

Some days he walked along making all the noise he could, whistling and hollering, hitting out at bushes with his rifle, stamping his feet on rocks, anything to ward off the big weight of the silence.

Other days he went along half holding his breath to keep from making a noise, because hearing anything at all in this enduring silence scared him most nigh to death. It was like the whole big countryside was waiting for him to make some sound, so it could tell where he was and come pouncing down on him.

He wished he could find some sign of white men, any kind of sign, a broken piggin or a thrown away ax helm or anything. He wasn't eager to see any Indian sign. But at least if he did, he would know he wasn't loose in the world all by himself, just one lone boy wandering and wandering and wandering without any other solitary soul left to see or hear him.

Walking along sometimes it would come over him that this was so, that his home and his pa and his ma, even the Worths and the Everys, all the other people in creation, were just things he'd made up his very own self. He'd never ever done another thing but pole up and down hills under these great trees, all by himself, never going anywhere, never coming from any place—on and on forevermore.

When that happened, sweat would break out all

over him, and he'd have to hold his rifle hard and mutter to himself and try to piece this thing together. He'd turn his shot pouch around and look at the place where his pa had burned his initials into it. There they were—K.B. He could remember that day so plain, it *must* be true; it couldn't help but be.

And then one morning he saw it—a blaze mark on a tree! A sign, and a sign of white men at that. Indians didn't blaze trees. Some white man had stripped off the bark there and cut three slashes above it, some farmer out to mark the borders of his land or show himself the way to a salt lick or something.

Kel could feel his face nigh split open with grinning. He reached up and touched the bare spot. It was dried out good, but not so old it had begun to darken. There were white folks around here, somewhere close!

He began to run, and it wasn't long till he reached a trail, faint and hard to see on the rocky ground, but a trace just the same. He sprinted along it, swinging his rifle high. He was home! In no time he'd be seeing his pa. He'd made it.

Suddenly there was a figure of a man up ahead,

just over a little rise. Before he could stop himself, Kel yelled out. The man swung around then, and Kel saw it was an Indian, a brave in war paint. Without thinking he swung his useless rifle to his shoulder.

The Indian stood in the trail with his legs spraddled out, raised his own gun, and leveled it at Kel.

10

Kel reckoned he could see straight down the Indian's rifle barrel, see the lead ball waiting at the bottom, ready to come whirling out straight at him. The savage was aiming for his head. The bullet would go right between his eyeballs and likely leave through the back of his skull, bringing his brains along with it. He could well nigh feel it hit, and he jerked his head back a little at the thought.

"Why don't he shoot?" Kel asked in agony. "How come he don't go ahead and shoot?"

The Indian's fingers pulled at the trigger.

With a howl Kel leapt from the path and ran. His pa always said that nothing greased a body's joints like being good and scared. Kel reckoned he was so scared, he'd outrun the bullet did the Indian shoot at him now. The trees were vast, the big butts stood wide apart, and there was little undergrowth. It was the best running country there was, and Kel sailed along like a deer in springtime.

He turned his head a little, and great day in the morning, the brave was running right alongside him, not a stone's throw away, leaping along as fast as a fire-singed wildcat! The savage saw him just at that moment. For a spell they ran along staring at each other. And then both runners stopped dead still.

Once again Kel swung his rifle to his shoulder, he couldn't seem to help himself. It was what a body did in time of danger.

The Indian, too, aimed his gun. Then he clawed frantically at his rifle, gave Kel a fearful look, and bounded off once more. Kel didn't move. He knew now how come he was standing there still alive and breathing. This time he'd seen how the lock of the Indian's rifle was all bound up with a dirty rag. It must be the brave had put it there to keep out the wet and plumb forgot it. He could have

pulled the trigger all day and Monday too, and the rifle wouldn't have fired, bundled up that way.

Kel grinned. There they had stood, each one waiting to be killed, each one with a no-good gun, each one scared witless of the other. He reckoned when he'd left the trail, feeling no call to stand there any longer, the red man had done the same thing. It just so happened that both of them had had the notion to run this way. So they had fled along, side by side, each one figuring he was leaving the other far behind.

The more he thought about it, the funnier it got to be. He rocked back and forth. He'd never in his life heard of anything so plumb foolish. Tears rolled down his face, and he got so weak, he had to sit down. Suddenly he didn't know whether he was laughing or crying. It had been a tarnal close call. Likely there were other Indians around here. The next one he met would be sure to have his rifle primed, ready to kill a lone white boy.

Kel took out a thin strip of his jerked meat and began to chew it slowly. It was tough as whit leather. It wouldn't have been so bad, only he was dry as the bottom of the bucket. Early that morning he'd shared a drink of cold spring water with

146

a pepper-breasted bird, but he'd come a long hot way through the summer day since then. Now it was all he could do to swallow.

There was a sudden sound of firing off to his right, sharp little pops, one after the other. It scared him, and he jumped as though he'd sat in hot ashes. The guns went on, a heap of them. He was pretty sure it was the Indians, after a fort. There couldn't be so much firing just to capture a lone settler's cabin.

"If there're whites around, I aim to join up with 'em," he said half aloud. Oh, he was aching for the sight of one of his own!

But he knew he'd have to be all-fired careful. No telling how many Indians were in these very woods, no telling where they might turn up next. They had ways of their own, and a body had best be pert and sharp-eyed.

Kel set off cautiously. The dim, greeny light under the big trees made things look strange. A bush was a crouching savage; a cluster of saplings might be a whole war party waiting to bash his head in. It made him skittish.

Just ahead of him a poplar tree had come down and taken a mess of young trees with it. Even with half of its roots sticking up in the air, it was still living, and the branches were heavy with leaves. A lot of the broken saplings had begun to shoot and sprout from their stumps.

That cave of living greenery would be a fine place for Indians to hide in, waiting to rush out and kill. Kel was just on the point of skirting away from it when he heard voices. He didn't hesitate a smidgin, just scuttled in among the poplar branches like a ground hog into a hole.

"Anybody hiding in here, better move over and make room for me," he told himself grimly. But there was no one in the leafy shelter.

The voices came closer. Through the sprouts Kel saw five Shawnee Indians, all in breechclouts and war paint, carrying rifles and all kinds of hatchets and knives. He held his breath, his body rigid. The ground under him was thick with dry leaves. One move and they would crackle like spring lightning and give him away.

The red men were arguing among themselves. Their voices rattled angrily. One of the braves stalked over to the windfall, close to Kel, and threw down his gun. Standing with arms folded, he gave the others a look of disgust.

The sight of him gave Kel a turn, for a fact. It wasn't just his being so close that Kel might have touched him. The man's body was covered with scars from head to foot. The skin on his face and neck was wrinkled and puckered. Burning made that, Kel knew, deep burning. He'd been cooked to a fare-thee-well, most nigh all over. There were places where knives had slashed and cut, and a hole as big as Kel's fist was in the front of his thigh. Kel knew what had happened to him. He'd been captured by some enemy tribe and put to the worst kind of torture.

"And that's what they'd do to me if'n they was to reach in here and lay hands on me," he thought miserably.

How come this warrior hadn't been all the way killed, Kel wondered? Had he endured so long and bravely that his enemies had taken pity on him? Maybe it was true, what he'd heard folks say, that Indians couldn't feel things the way white men did. His eyes lingered on the pit in the man's leg. You'd have to be dead before you didn't feel having a piece of meat that size gouged out of you.

One thing sure, if he got captured, Kel hoped

it wasn't by this brave. He would know too well how to kill a body by the littlest bits and pieces.

Midges swarmed around Kel's eyes and nose. He longed to wave them off. But the worst was when he made sure he was going to sneeze. He put up his hand, softly, softly, and pinched his nose to keep the sneeze back. It worked, but he well nigh throttled himself. His tongue had the dry swells, and he just couldn't seem to suck in enough air through his mouth. He let go his nose and prayed the Indians would go away.

The scarred warrior scooped up his rifle and without a glance at the others strode off ahead of them. Kel waited till he was sure they weren't coming back; then he crawled out. He had to find some water or perish plumb away. But he couldn't just go running around looking. These woods belonged to the Shawnee. He'd have to push on softly and trust to luck on the water.

The only thing wet he chanced upon was a little pool in a hollow stump. Mrs. Every used to say such water was poisonous, but little she knew. He'd drunk it before without dying, and he meant to do it now, though it was ringed with frogstools, and there was a hairy sort of worm lying drowned at the bottom.

Bringing his face down, he drank. The water was warm and flat, but he didn't care. He'd have drunk mud just to slicken up his tongue again. He straightened up and wiped his mouth on his sleeve. It came over him how tired he was. His eyes burned in his head, and his hand trembled just a little. The day was only half gone. The rest of it stretched in front of him, and he had a feeling it wasn't going to be easy to get through.

"I got to find the fort, first off," he told himself. "Then a good hidey-hole to wait in till dark."

He glanced about. There wasn't enough cover in these woods to hide a pig's grunt. A hoptoad or a possum might find cover here with no worriment but not a nigh-grown boy. If it wasn't so dangerous tramping about, he'd go back to the windfall. But who could tell what these fool savages were up to or whether they had scouts out or a camping place nearabout? He couldn't take any chances. There wasn't any point in coming this far piece from Virginny just to let some redskin sneak up and blow him full of holes.

The woods were still. He listened so hard, he reckoned his ears must be standing out from his head. He put one cautious foot after another. He had to make himself move away from one tree out into the open and across to the next big trunk. It was slow, jumpy progress, but he pushed on. He watched every side; he even walked backward for spells. It worried him that he could be here in the middle of the savages and yet see so little sign of them. And not a whoop had he heard out of them. It was strange, and he didn't like it.

All at once the firing rattled up again, right in front of him. It gave him a jolt, it was so close. He swallowed hard and kept on going, slipping in and out. Soon he could see what looked like a clearing ahead of him. The sight almost made him forget the danger. On hands and knees he crawled out of the trees through the weeds to the very edge of the field, and there, across an acre of stumps, was a fort.

He just about shouted out. It was small, but it looked bold and proud, crowning the rise that way, with its blockhouses and its spiky palisade all around it and the chimneys sticking up cheerfully from the cabins inside. The shooting had ceased, but smoke still drifted from one of the loopholes. Kel's eyes filled with tears. Maybe his pa had fired that gun through the fort wall. The thought made him weak and mollicobbled inside.

He longed to see some other sign of white men. But in the hot noon sun the place lay silent and quiet, though once he thought he heard a dog bark inside. He took everything in carefully. The gate stood almost directly in front of him. The slope up to it was dotted with low stumps like warts on a toad's back. Tonight he could make his way up that hill, he could slip from stump to stump, he could get to the gate and knock, and someone would let him in. He'd be home; he'd be safe. He let the feeling of it run over him, like the heat from a fire on a cold morning. It was so close, so close.

Oh, he could have stayed there the rest of the livelong day, hoping for a sight of somebody along the parapet at the wall's top, a brown rifle barrel poked through a loophole, anything to let him know folks were there. But he had a peg of sense left. He had to get away from here.

He looked all around and caught the gleam of a sycamore a little ways from him. It looked to have been dead a right good while and might likely be hollow. Half stooping, he made for it through the thick undergrowth along the rim of the field.

The tree was hollow. Woodpeckers had whacked away at its top, and owls had nested there, for their pellets lay all about on the ground. There was a wopsided opening at the foot, and Kel slid inside. It wasn't roomy enough to stretch out, but the trunk was rotted out way above his head, and he could stand with ease.

Looking down, he wished the opening wasn't quite so wide. He had an uneasy notion whoever passed by could see a white boy's feet and legs sprouting up inside that tree. He scrounged over to one side and shuffled up the dead wood into the hole and hoped he was hidden.

With a yawn he sank down and sat hugging his knees. Red harvestmen and varmints with near about a million legs scurried over his feet. Dust and cobwebs hung in the still air and made it hard to breathe. He was hungry again, but he was scared to try the last of his meat. Thirsty as he was, he'd choke himself on the dried morsel. He dozed in the heat, and when he woke, his clothes were soaked with sweat.

A ray of sunlight slanted down through the motes, and he glanced up. A few feet above his head was a sort of window, a hole in the trunk where a limb had decayed and fallen away.

"I could get up there and see out," he told himself. "It had ought to be some fresh air there anyway." It would be something to do to pass away the time.

The wood was soft, and footholds were easy to cut. The space narrowed as he went up, so he was wedged in by the time he reached his lookout. Still, it wasn't too bad, just tight enough to give him some support besides the scanty steps he had dug out to put his toes in.

As he settled himself at the hole, the tree swayed back and forth. It scared him. Then he thought he must have imagined it. It could be he was a mite dizzy or not good and awake yet. He rubbed at his eyes and pulled his face up close to the window.

A shiny green June bug was there before him. Pushing it away with his finger, he looked out. There was the fort, still showing no signs of anybody inside. He studied it for a while, piecing out in his mind just which fort it might be. He decided it must be Logan's. Folks on the trail had said there weren't but three forts left in all Kentuck. Boonesborough and Harrodsburg were big places with lots of cabins. This one, for all its gallant look, was small. It couldn't have more than fifteen-twenty riflemen inside.

And one of them was his pa, he knew in reason. How he longed to see that old wool hat Pa wore and that grin. His pa had the best grin in all creation. Folks back in Wolf Hills always said his grin was so wide, he couldn't get through a cabin door head on; no sir, his pa had to turn sideways to get inside with it. Oh, it seemed a shame that a man like that should have a coward for a son, a coward and a deserter.

The cooler, sweeter air was almost as good as a drink of water. Kel stayed there, for the longest time, not anxious to lower himself into the stuffy depths of the trunk. Yet there was nothing to look at. Not a soul stirred; the leaves of the trees drooped in the heat. Even the sun hung unmoving in the thick blue of the sky. And then he saw the Indians, three of them, slipping along like turkeys in tall grass, one after another, and heading his way.

Quickly Kel drew back from the hole, though

he didn't think they could see him. It pleased him that he was hidden so well. They came along grunting to each other, their moccasined feet slapping along over the packed ground. They had no call to be careful, here out of range of the fort rifles, with nobody hunting them.

They came closer and passed out of his sight under the tree. When next he saw them, there were only two going off into the woods. Whatever had happened to the other one? He raised himself to try to see below. There was the warrior studying the ground around the sycamore.

Kel's heart began to race. Something was poking about in the trunk. He sucked in his belly and stared down into the dusky space at the tree's bottom. A rifle barrel was being jabbed this way and that. His legs went so weak, he all but fell. His hiding place had been discovered. In a moment the brave would find his rifle and shot bag lying there on the mat of dead wood and know a white boy was holed up in this sycamore.

11

Like a long finger the rifle barrel prodded and pried and thumped around inside the sycamore. Any moment it would go clanging against his own gun, Kel knew. He shrank away from the sound as he might cower from a blow, but it didn't come. After a year and a day, the Indian drew out his rifle.

Kel dug his fingers into the soft wood on either side of him. Relief made his knees even weaker than fear. It was all he could do to cling there and not go racketing down to the ground. But he held on. He would stick there till the savage was out of earshot; he had to.

After a while he peeked out of the hole. The Shawnee hadn't gone away. He was squatting there, still as a bury box, with his rifle across his knees.

"How come he don't go packing off?" thought Kel desperately. "He ain't found nothing in this here tree. How come he don't take off?"

Yet he knew the answer. The Indian was waiting for him to come down. Likely he'd found tracks leading right into this tree. Likely he knew clear as light that it was a white boy, scared almost witless, hiding here. Kel groaned silently. He'd been so busy watching for redskins, he hadn't given a thought to covering his trail. Now his trifling ways had found him out.

The Indian could outwait him. Savages had the knack of sitting patient and still for days, if need be, to kill an enemy. This brave had a good comfortable place to wait. He wasn't jammed into a tree trunk with his feet resting mostly on empty air, struggling to keep himself balanced.

"I might as well give up," Kel told himself. "I might as well let him kill me now as wait till I'm half dead."

He could talk about giving up, but he didn't

159

aim to do it. He knew in reason he would cling there till he dropped. Giving up was a thing he hardly even knew how to do.

Shifting about, he tried to make himself a little more secure. One of his feet began to cramp. An iron knot of pain ran up his calf. He opened his mouth in a soundless gasp of misery while his muscles bunched and the snarling agony tore at him like an animal. Sweat ran down his body, and he pressed his face into the rotten wood to keep from yelling out.

At last the cramping stopped. He sagged against the tree, and it creaked threateningly. He held his breath, thinking surely the Shawnee had heard.

But it didn't make any difference, did it? The brave knew he was in here and was just waiting for Kel to use up the last least drop of his strength before twisting a forked stick into his hide and hauling him out like some forest varmint to be killed with a rap on the head.

The hot still afternoon crawled by. Kel stared out of the hole, halfway not knowing what he was doing there, not even sure where he was. He could believe he was asleep and dreaming. He couldn't seem to make his head work properly; his thoughts kept lolloping off with the Worths' cows. Everything was strange and jumbled up, and he kept thinking this was some other time and some other place.

He had a powerful thirst; that was real enough. It was so blamed hot. The sky was hazy, but there was no rain in it, he could tell, just more dust and heat. Something out of all reason had happened to this day to make it three times longer than most days, to keep him roasting over a slow fire of weariness and thirst and misery.

The Indian stood up. Kel jerked back from his opening and tried to silence his hot, crackling breath. It was a queer thing, the way he kept acting like the Shawnee didn't know he was there. There was always the chance that was the truth, he reckoned. Now, snatched out of his stupor, feeling his aching muscles and his swollen dry mouth and the itching torment of the heat, he still hoped. He still waited for dark to come and give him a chance to slip down and away.

He glanced at the fort. "Pa," he thought suddenly. "How come you don't come get me? How come you ain't run out to help me?"

Oh, he was forevermore addled, thinking that

way. As far as his pa knew, he was dead or back in Wolf Hills. There was nobody to help him. Likely if the folks in the station knew he was here, they wouldn't come out. Why should they? Had he offered to help others at the risk of his skin? Not Kel Bond. He'd just stood there and let his friends get slaughtered. Just stood there . . .

It would serve him right if the Injuns killed him. He deserved it, but he wasn't going to let it happen. He was going to get out of here; he had to. He had to get up that slope and tell his pa that his son was a coward and a no-good. He didn't want his father going around bragging about having a good, decent son when it wasn't true, not a word of it. That would make things worse than ever.

"I aim to hang on," he told the Shawnee grimly. "I mean to stick here till dark, and then I mean to get away. I got to."

He wasn't thinking straight. His brains had likely cooked in his head. But he knew as truly as he knew his name was Kelsey Bond that he was honor bound not to let go but to last out and get away from this savage so that he could tell his pa the bitter truth.

The sun was setting. At first he thought it was just the haze thickening. He couldn't rightly credit that the day was going to end. But it was. The light grew dimmer and dimmer, and on the long rise up to the fort, the stumps grew bigger and bigger with their own dark images.

He stared as hard as he could. He hoped to remember where the biggest stumps were, the ones that could shelter a boy worn down to thumb size and hide him from the Injuns till he could scurry up to the gate and beg to be let in. He stared till lights flashed in front of his eyes, and he had to press his feverish cheek against the rotted wood.

He shifted his gaze to the Indian. The brave was still standing, not ten feet from the sycamore. He was looking off to the left, into the dusk. Of a sudden, swiftly, silently, in one long easy motion, he went to one knee and pulled his cocked rifle to his shoulder. Kel turned his head.

A white man was coming. In the twilight he was creeping along the edge of the clearing, carrying his rifle at the ready. But he kept looking behind him, as though he saw or felt someone there. He didn't scan the woods in Kel's direction. He wore no hat, his hair was clubbed back with string, and he seemed to be a young fellow, hardly a grown man.

What was he doing out of doors here? Had he gone for help? Had he gone to shoot game and fetch it back? Whatever his errand, if he didn't look sharp, he wasn't going to make it. Another few steps and he'd be so close, the Shawnee couldn't miss.

The white man raised a cautious foot. Kel could almost hear the Indian's finger tighten on that trigger. He pushed against the tree, and all his muscles tensed.

This way, Kel's heart wailed, look this way quick.

But the man wouldn't. And all at once Kel was shouting in a thick, dry voice, "Run, run! Watch out!"

There was a terrible harsh, rending noise. Kel had a curious feeling of flying, and then he hit the ground with a stunning smack. The breath flew out of him, and for a minute he couldn't see or hear for the roaring trapped inside his head.

Then he was climbing out of the split shell of the sycamore, throwing off slivers of wood and broken limbs. His legs ached like sin and were almost too shaky to hold him up. Pieces of the tree lay all around, and the Shawnee was crumpled up under one of the limbs. Kel could see it had whopped him a good blow.

He stood there, swaying, shaking his head, well nigh insensible. The Indian moved and opened his eyes. He saw Kel then, and his face squeezed together. He fumbled for the knife at his side and finally managed to pull it loose. With it in his hand he got to his knees.

Kel grabbed up a stick. Desperately he whacked out and hit the redskin over the head. The limb broke. The warrior groaned and slumped forward. The boy looked around for his rifle. There it was with the shot pouch in the broken stump. He grabbed them and fled unsteadily into the shadows. He'd gone some little ways through the trees before he realized he was headed in the wrong direction.

Whirling around, he slipped off toward the clearing. He didn't hear or see a thing. Why hadn't the other savages come pounding up at the commotion? And what had become of the white man?

He reached the clearing and rested there at the edge, getting his breath. It was dark as pitch, the way a cloudy summer night can get all of a sud-

den. He couldn't see a thing; yet it felt as though anybody could see him. Eyes stared at him from every direction, and he bobbed and jumped every which way. He stood out like a red bird on a snowy day; he knew he did.

He took a good grip on his rifle. The cold touch of the metal calmed him. "I got to quit this," he told himself. "Can't nobody see me. But they can sure hear me squirming around."

He wished he had something to drink. His throat and mouth were so dry, he couldn't swallow good. The least little thing might set him coughing.

Standing up, he stepped out into the clearing. Overhead the sky was deep and troubled with clouds. Not a star shone.

Not a crack of light shone from the station either. Oh, you could tell his pa had had a hand in building those cabins, lined up in the stockade. Somebody had worked hard to make those strong, solid walls so no bullet or arrow could find a crack to slip through, so the face they turned toward the enemy was firm and unyielding.

But right now he wished he could make out a chink or a cranny, a flicker of firelight or candle flame to guide him and keep him company.

He went forward slowly, feeling for the stumps so as not to trip and fall and bring the savages down on him. A night this dark, the redskins wouldn't be in the woods. They'd be scurrying around here, surely, out to see what devilment they could do under the cover of blackness.

A little stir of air fanned his cheek, and he whipped around, thinking to see a Shawnee with a tomahawk standing over him. But it was only an owl, hawking over the slope after mice or moles.

A fox barked and a whippoorwill called.

Kel wondered did those varmints wear redskins and breechclouts? He had a notion they did. But for a fact they were lonesome sounds, the little sharp yelp and the high, sad voices of the night birds. They were sounds a body might hear as he lay dying.

Thunder rumbled in the west. Thirsty as he was, he hoped it didn't rain. This clearing would be hip deep with mud and so slick, he'd never make it up. He was going to have the devil's own time reaching the fort and finding the gate as it was.

He went on. Every time he came to a stump, he got the willycobbles, thinking each black hump might not be a stump but a crouching Indian. And each time he touched the rough axed surface, his hand lingered, glad of a reminder of safety ahead among his own kind.

He was headed uphill, he was sure. And that must be the fort, that dark shape before him. He hurried his steps, and his foot slipped on wood chips, and he fell. The noise was as loud as the thunder that came and went overhead. On his belly he got away quick, pushing his rifle before him, sliding up and up. All at once he was there. Under his hands he felt the rough bark of the pickets. He huddled there with his head leaning against the logs. He was home.

Now all he had to do was find the gate and get inside. In the darkness he hadn't the least idea which was the gate side.

"I'll just have to go along till I find it," he thought.

With one hand on the wall, he stumbled off. The stockade ended, and one of the snug-built cabins began. There would be folks inside, sleeping safe and sound. He knew in reason there wouldn't be a shuttered window, but he hoped. He aimed to call and let these fort folks know he was out here needing a power of help.

It was a silly notion. A shout loud enough to wake the sleepers would bring the Injuns a-running. When they finished with him, he wouldn't need a way inside. No, the thing to do was find the gate. There would be guards there, bound to be. They'd hear him and let him in, did he only whisper.

The cabin gave way to fence and then another cabin set at the corner. There was a sudden flash of heat lightning, and he cowered against the palisade. Had someone seen him? Friend or foe, they might shoot him, not knowing what he was doing there against the fort wall.

In the blackness he hurried on, feeling, feeling for the gate. A turn and down another side of cabins and more logs, all crowded tight together. He began to worry that he had missed the gate, hurrying along like he was. Had he been around two corners now or was it three? The lightning flickered but not bright enough to show him a thing.

Frantically he rushed forward, his hands exploring the fence. There was no opening, just a solid wall of logs. He had missed the gate. He'd have to go around again. This time he'd make sure he found it. The fence was set upright in the ground, but the gate wouldn't be. He stooped and went feeling along the ground. It was dusty. His breath whistled in and out of his dry mouth till he almost choked.

Then he found it. The gate, the gate! The fine wide planks and the space underneath. He beat on the wood with his gun, and it rattled faintly. Nobody could hear that, he knew. He banged harder, looking around behind him, scared and trembling.

Somebody stirred inside. "What was that?" asked a voice.

Another voice answered, "I didn't hear nothing. Maybe the wind's getting up. There's a storm somewhere."

Now was the time to call out. They were there, ready and waiting for him. Kel opened his mouth and yelled, "Let me in, let me in."

But no words came out, only a rasping rattle. He was too dry; he couldn't speak. He tried to wet his lips, but his mouth was parched and juiceless. With his finger he scrouged around at his tongue. It felt thick and stiff as a gunstock.

A third voice spoke, "I was checking along the wall loopholes. Thought I seen somebody outside in a lightning flash back a ways."

"It was me, Kelsey Bond. Help me. Let me in

quick," Kel cried out in his gasping voice, but it was the sound of dried corn stalks in a high wind.

Once more he beat on the gate with his gun.

"If'n there's somebody out there, holler out," cried someone.

The lightning looped across the sky. Oh, can't they see me, Kel agonized in his mind? Can't they see it's me?

But what would they see when they looked out? A wild, ragged, woodsy creature, skinny and dirty, with hair to his shoulders and clothes that were no more than a decent way of going naked. They wouldn't know he was a white boy with an honest father inside with them.

The lightning flickered on and off, as steady as a heart beat now, smothering the hilltop in a strange dancing pallor. As Kel beat at the gate again, he glanced over his shoulder. He was sure one of the stumps was creeping up the slope. The Indians had heard all this racket. If he wasn't taken in soon, it would be too late.

"Don't take down them bars," a man ordered. "Them red varmints are up to some trick, I'll wager. Open that gate a pin crack, and they'll be in here like the milltails of trouble."

A shadow glided along the wall, a shadow with a tomahawk in its hand. The blade burned and gleamed in the fluttering light. Kel beat at his jaw, rubbed at his throat, trying desperately to shake loose his voice. There was nothing for him to do but keep pounding on the gate.

There was a hubbub inside the fort. "Injuns." "Get to your places." "Pettit, fetch a piggin of water." "Is the gate on fire?" "Let 'em come!" Then a long whoop sounded, different from the fighting kind the Indians gave but just as wild and loud.

"They'll see me and this Injun and think we're both savages," Kel thought. He had to do something and that mighty dern quick. He had to let these white folks know some way that he was one of them.

Suddenly Kel lowered his rifle till it rested against his thigh. Taking his knife in his right hand, he slashed at his other arm. He hardly felt the sting of it. In the pale flashes of lightning the blood looked black. Kel pressed his lips against the wound and drank the warm salty liquid. His throat was so dry, it would hardly work. But his mouth was wet, and his thickened tongue was

173

loosened. He sucked more of his blood till his cracked throat opened.

"Let me in quick," he yelled. "It's me, Kelsey Bond. My pa's here!"

The Indian was on him. He could smell the rancid bear grease. "Help me, help me!" he screamed, falling back from the naked figure that loomed up over him.

There was running inside the fort and more shouted orders. A torch came sailing over the pickets. In its glaring light Kel saw the Shawnee draw back his hatchet. Kel struck out with the stock of his gun. He hit the brave as hard as he could, but he knew it wasn't much of a blow. He was too tired and scared to have any strength left.

The Indian grabbed his rifle and tried to wrench it from his hand. Kel held on tight and was slammed against the wall. The warrior wadded up the boy's loose shirt in his fist and shook him so hard, his head banged on the logs. By the guttering torchlight Kel saw the tomahawk. It hung there in the dimness above him, a live thing ready to split his head wide open. He couldn't move; the Indian had him wedged against the fence. He screamed, and his muscles turned to sand. Nothing would save him.

There was a terrible explosion somewhere. The hatchet started toward him and suddenly tumbled from the brave's hand and glanced off Kel's shoulder. The savage collapsed half on top of him. Someone seized him from behind and dragged him through an opening in the gate so narrow that it well nigh skinned him.

He looked up, and there stood his father. He wondered for a minute if it were true. And then he knew it was.

"Pa," he said, "I come on to Kentuck, like you told me to."

12

The rifle shot echoed and echoed in the still woods. It seemed to bounce from one big tree trunk to another. The deer leaped once and fell. When Kel ran toward it, he could see its legs twitch a mite, and then it was dead.

It was hot. August dog days always were. Under the trees the air was thick and warm like water in a stew pot. Gnats swarmed everywhere.

But gnats were a sight better to have swarming around than Injuns, Kel told himself. He had arrived at the fort the last day of May. Since then they hadn't been much troubled with Indians.

Everybody said the Shawnees would be back, and

Kel didn't doubt it, but right this minute the woods were safe as apple cider.

A good thing too, for there were no crops to speak of and no cattle left alive. Game was their chief source of food, and it had to be eaten without salt or bread. Nobody complained about the lack of vittles. It was good not to be penned up inside the walls, all crowded together. Kel and his pa had hunted every chance they got, and once Kel had even had a shot at a buffalo, but he'd missed.

He hadn't missed this buck, however. He was kneeling by it with his knife in his hand when his pa came up.

"That was a mighty pretty shot," Mr. Bond said. "I seen it from over there a ways. A fine shot and a fine kill. We'll have us a nice hide out of that."

Kel looked up and smiled. It had been a good shot, he knew. He'd wheeled at the first leap of the buck and shot offhand, half expecting his lead ball to sail wide. But it hadn't, and his pa had seen. When you did something well, Pa always saw it and pointed it out and was as pleased over it as if he'd done it his very own self.

Now Kel went back to his skinning, sliding the knife down the legs. "We going home now?" he asked. "Or do you aim to try for another deer?"

"We'll go home," Pa answered. "I reckon if we was to hap on any game, we wouldn't pass it by. But this'll meat us for a good spell, and we can take a haunch to Mrs. Puwitt."

Mrs. Puwitt had lost her husband in the siege. A bullet had struck him in the ribs, not a bad wound, but a piece of the ball had broken off in him and stayed inside. The place had festered and swollen and got worse and worse, so that Mr. Puwitt was wild with fever, and there wasn't anything anybody could do for him. He had finally died.

"I'm like Mr. Puwitt," thought Kel suddenly. "There's a piece of something in me that fevers and hurts all the time. It seems like it ought to poison me to death just any day now."

He squatted there holding the knife and looking off into the woods and thinking this. He forgot about Pa and the deer and Mrs. Puwitt, just thinking about the fiery lump inside him. He was a coward. He had deserted his friends in need. It was a queer thing. He'd come all that long way

178

through the wilderness, planning to tell his pa all about it. Even if his pa ranted and raved and cuffed him, the way he'd seen a mean-tempered man do his boy once, Kel figured it would be a thing he deserved. No matter what happened, if he just told his pa the truth, inside he would be better off. It would be like a poultice on an open sore; it would soothe and help.

And he had told his pa the truth, every bit of it. Right out in front of all the fort folks he had said, "Them two woodsies I traveled a ways with got killed. I could of helped them, but I didn't. I was too scared."

He'd spelled it out, loud and clear, and nobody had paid any mind. Nobody had said a thing.

"I reckon they was sorry for my pa was the reason," Kel told himself. "It's terrible hard, having a boy like that. They knew and were too mannerly to say a thing."

But they thought shame of him, Kel was sure. He couldn't meet their eyes. He kept away from the other boys in the fort as much as he could. And now that the siege was over and he didn't have to be with folks, he went everywhere with his pa, stuck to him like a prickle bur. The others wouldn't want him around; he knew that well enough. Out of the corner of his eyes he'd watched them, and he'd seen how they watched his every move with hateful, sneering looks, scornful of a boy who hadn't been able to stand up to danger.

"What ails you, Kel?" asked Mr. Bond suddenly. "You see something?"

Kel jumped. "Naw," he answered quickly. "I was just thinking." He began to saw away at the deer, not looking at his father.

"Here," said Mr. Bond finally. "You ain't skinning that buck. You're fixing to make whangs out of it. That's a good pelt. Take care with it."

Kel handed him the knife. "You do it," he said. "I can't put my mind to it."

Mr. Bond took the knife and swiftly stripped the hide from the flesh. "Well, that's a true word," he said. "I been watching you. Whatever you got your mind on, it ain't around here. You spend a heap of time wool-gathering, seems like."

Kel said nothing.

Mr. Bond sat back on his heels and looked at his son. "I've had it in mind to ask you," he went on at last, "ask you did you want to go back to Wolf Hills?"

"Wolf Hills?" gasped Kel. "The Everys? Whatever for?"

Then he looked away. He knew what for. His pa didn't want him with him. His pa was a brave man and an important one in the fort. It stood to reason he wouldn't like having a son who was a weakling and a coward trailing him all around everywhere.

"I'll go back," Kel said sadly. "Any time you can find a way for me to go, I'll go."

Mr. Bond bent over the deer's carcass, working out the liver and some strips along the spine. "It'll be a while yet afore I can find a way for you to go," he said in a few minutes. "I hadn't put much thought to it. I reckon I didn't rightly think you would want to go. Seems like you had so much trouble getting here, you would of stayed on."

Once again Kel was silent.

"How come you made that journey anyhow?" Pa said. "If'n you didn't want to be with me, how come you just didn't send a message? Or anyway, how come you didn't stay with the cow people since you figured they'd turn back?"

Kel stood up. "I wanted to come," he almost shouted. "Oh, you never thought I didn't want to come? I'd a heap rather be here than back in Wolf Hills! But I ain't fixing to let you be shamed of me. I don't aim to let folks think bad of you because of me."

"Shamed of you!" cried Mr. Bond. "I was proud. You come all that way by yourself, and a body could see it took grit and gimption. You wasn't hardly more than ramrod-size when you got here. It ain't many boys could of done it."

Kel put his face in his hands. "I was a coward," he squeaked out. "I wouldn't go help them two fellers. I let the Injuns kill 'em."

There was a stillness in the greeny twilight of the woods. Nobody said anything more. Kel took his hands down. His father was cutting the second haunch from the deer's back.

Finally Mr. Bond spoke. "Luke McClemore was through here night before last," he said. "He was telling about how you shouted out and saved his hide that night when he come by the fort and you was up in the tree."

Kel nodded. He remembered all right.

"You was lucky," Mr. Bond continued. "It might of been the last thing you ever did. That Injun could of killed you easy."

"I—I wasn't brave," Kel said miserably. "If'n you're trying to make me think I was brave, I wasn't. I never went to holler out; I just did it without hardly knowing I was doing it. I couldn't help it."

"Well, it may be you couldn't of helped not running to fight with them woodsies," Mr. Bond pointed out. "Do you think you could of?"

"I don't know," cried out Kel. "I couldn't make my legs work to go find out. They just wouldn't run, somehow."

"Then I reckon you couldn't help it," said Mr. Bond. "It wasn't you was the coward; it was just your legs."

Kel pondered.

"Oh, it ain't the easiest thing ever to live with the notion that you didn't help when you might of," Mr. Bond added. "But there ain't a man I know of hasn't done something in his life he wished he hadn't. Or not done something that he wished he had. It's a thing a person has to learn about himself. It makes him try a heap harder, so if he learns this early, he's got a lot of time to do his hard trying in."

He began to strap up the meat for carrying, wrapping the skin around it.

"I learned a long while back not to fault anybody for a thing like that. It might be I wouldn't of been able to make my legs work either," he stated finally. "A man don't know what he can or can't do till he tries, and you tried. That's all a body can ask."

He smiled at Kel suddenly. "And see here, you tried almighty hard to come to Kentuck, and you did it, though many a growed man would have turned back or just give up and died."

Was it true, Kel wondered? He hadn't thought he'd been brave to come on. He'd just thought about getting to his pa. He'd known it was wrong to give up, not to keep on trying, but he hadn't thought it was a brave thing to do.

But maybe it had been. Maybe the bravest things were the things you did without knowing you were being brave, without expecting other people to know you were brave.

Mr. Bond didn't say anything more. He bundled up the deer meat so he could carry it, gave Kel his rifle, and they set off through the hot afternoon. They walked for half an hour without speaking, till they came to the foot of the slope and the stockade loomed above them.

"And you know," Mr. Bond spoke again suddenly, "I reckon your legs were right not to take you into that fight. You'd of got killed sure. You wouldn't of come to Kentuck."

They reached the fort and walked under the raised gate. Mr. Bond swung his load of meat to the ground in front of the two-story blockhouse where the single men stayed.

"Them woodsies, they lived by the woods, and they figured to die by the woods," he declared. "You couldn't have helped. There was too many Injuns." He turned to the boy and asked, his voice sharp, "You know what folks are already calling this year, 1777? You know?"

Kel nodded. The Year of the Bloody Sevens. The year was nowhere near over, and folks had already tied on a tag to it. It was a year they'd not put out of their minds for a long time, if ever. So many had already died in the battles with the Indians, so many had already felt the savages' scalping knives and tomahawks and carried forever the red marks of this year, so much blood had already been sent splashing over the Kentucky soil to soak in and darken it that it was a wonder any were left who cared to stay on. Never before was such a year known.

"Too many folks have give up and left. Too many lie quiet underground," Mr. Bond exclaimed. "We need every man we can get here in Logan's Fort. We needed you, Kel, needed you bad. A heap of folks took heart when they saw how a lone young 'un had come that long, hard way just to get here. Like I say, you ain't ever going to forget Carr and Horne, and I don't want you to forget 'em. But another thing you got to remember is, if'n you had got killed, who'd of been here to shoot this deer to give to Mrs. Puwitt and her boy chaps? Now take this haunch and skedaddle over there to her cabin."

Kel skedaddled.

As he crossed the fort yard, he thought things over. He reckoned he wasn't going to die of his bullet fester after all. It was going to leave a scar and a big knotty lump, like the one Hoke Carr had had in his leg where an arrowhead was still in him.

But it wasn't going to kill him, he knew now. Anyway, not right away. Not till he helped his pa build a farm in Kentucky. Not till he brought Mrs. Puwitt the meat she needed with no man of her own to shift for her. Not till the war with the Indians was over and the fort torn down and he had done every living thing he could to make this a good place to live, with folks and cabins, fenced-in fields of corn and shucky beans and turnips.

Would he be brave enough to do all that had to be done? All of a sudden he didn't care. He was brave enough to try. He was certain of that anyway.

"Hi, Mrs. Puwitt," he sang out. "We brung you a nice smack of deer meat!"